How I Saved a Planet!

Publisher's Note to the Reader

This manuscript was discovered, handwritten and dog-eared, in an abandoned storage unit in Upstate New York. The author could not be located, and, after much deliberation, the decision was made to publish the story as written, with no alterations. We should like to note that we do not necessarily endorse the author's views, nor have we validated the accuracy of the events he claims to have experienced.

Due to the bizarre and sometimes inscrutable nature of the writing, a few explanatory and apologetic editor's notes have been sprinkled sparingly throughout the work. Our hope is that you enjoy this strange tale despite its flaws.

Chapter A

I hadn't expected that. I really hadn't. It's not every day that you see a head detach so easily from a body and go rolling across the floor. There was no blood. How could there be no blood? A tense, awkward silence filled the pod as I stood frozen in shock. *What the hell just happened?* I couldn't help but stare in speechless awe at my hand—was it really that powerful? I wouldn't have thought so, but the twitching, headless body crumpled on the floor in front of me said otherwise.

How did I get to this point? I asked myself, my hand trembling. My mind wandered back to the events that had led to—haha, just kidding. My thoughts didn't go anywhere but to that rolling head. I'm trying to transition into meaningful backstory here, but I'm failing to summon a good segue. See, a hook was necessary to drag you into my story, but now I must back up and tell this tale from the beginning, else it will make no sense. (It probably won't make much sense anyway, but I'll leave that up to you.)

Now, in the unlikely event that this manuscript of my adventure is found, read, appreciated, and published, I have a couple stipulations. Firstly, things must be printed exactly as they are written. No changes. No alterations for "flow" or "cohesion" or whatever foolish reason publishers see fit to mangle books these days. Secondly, should it be deemed desirable to put this story into audio format (for reasons that I can't imagine), I should prefer that it be read by someone with a commandingly rich yet mysterious voice, with a touch of the sinister. (A short list of names comes to mind…)

But I digress. You were wanting to know the sequence of events that led to the horrific opening of this tale. Well, here goes nothing.

π π π π π

My life sucked balls. It really did. Here I was, just finished with freshman year at college, and I was driving back to spend the summer at Mom's house. This is what happens when you are a poor student with no money for a vacation or your own apartment and your deadbeat father is off on some tropical island with his whore of a girlfriend. Yes, getting stuck with Mom for an entire summer is what happens.

It didn't matter though. I was going to enjoy myself. I wasn't going to think about my dad enjoying the bright sun and the beautiful ocean. I wasn't going to think about all the tanning and all the midnight swims and all the wonderful food. I wasn't going to think about him lying in the warm sand, feeding juicy strawberries to topless supermodels—their sun-kissed skin glistening and their wet hair clinging to their curvaceous bodies, moist lips agape and eyes sparkling with mischief and anticipation. Oops, the strawberries are dripping. Allow me to lick it off…

Yeah, I wasn't going to think about any of that.

After telling myself what I wasn't going to be thinking about, the next step was to figure out exactly what to do with myself. You have to understand, I grew up in a small town. Like, really small. Bedford Falls and Bomont were giant metropolises compared to our little…place. We shared a school and a church with the next town over. (Of course they would get the only decent supermarket in the area. Our

To my darling, Georgie, without whose encouragement, support, and love this book would have never been possible.

How I Saved a Planet!

Or: The Strange Tale of How I Was Summoned from Earth to Help Save Another Planet from Destruction and the Many Weird and Wonderful Creatures, Places, and Events I Encountered During My Trip and...Oops Now I'm All Out of Space, So Fuck It

Stephen Quatro

Carteret, New Jersey

Printed in the United States of America

First Edition, 2020

ISBN 978-1-7346015-0-3 (paperback)
ISBN 978-1-7346015-1-0 (MOBI e-book)
ISBN 978-1-7346015-2-7 (EPUB e-book)

Library of Congress Control Number: 2020902940

4Qorners Press
www.4QornersPress.com

Cover design by Saad Ali, Covers by Creatives
Editing by Kimberly See, www.kimberlysee.com

"supermarket" was a 7-Eleven.) We only had one bar—well, half a bar really. It was the upstairs to the laundromat. Our gas station had a single pump…

You get the idea. Our town was small. And had no one my age. I mean literally no one. Not even close. I think you had to sign a pact before moving in that you would have absolutely, positively no children while living there. My parents disobeyed, obviously; leave it to them. And now here I was driving back to that boring place.

I pulled into the driveway, turned off the car, and sat there, staring miserably at this place I used to call home. 27 Sickamore Street. *Blah.* The house was just as drab as I remembered it. Light gray siding, dark gray shutters, a black front door—*who the hell designed this place?* I thought, shaking my head. At least the neighbor's house was all brown; clearly, he was moving up in the world. With an eye-roll to the heavens, I lumbered reluctantly out of the car and grabbed my belongings. It was an unseasonably chilly gray evening, and I shivered a bit as I headed toward the front door.

For sake of time, and to spare you the boredom I was plagued with, I'll skim over the next few events. Basically, my mom greeted me warmly, we had dinner and chatted, I was set up in my old bedroom, Mom went downstairs to bake brownies, I was left alone to unpack, etc., etc.

After unpacking, I sat down at my old desk and stared out the window. Same window, same view as always: the empty parking lot across the street, the abandoned store it belonged to, the row of houses on the street behind it, the old rusty water tower across town in the distance. Nothing had changed.

Nothing but the person staring at it all.

College hadn't been as fulfilling or exciting as I had hoped it would be. I had struggled in the beginning to pick a major that suited me, and I felt intimidated by my peers, who seemed to have their futures mapped out so perfectly. Some of my classes had proved interesting, but most of my time was spent going through the motions, unsure of everything except how miserable I was.

I didn't even want to think about what would happen when college ended. Would I end up back here, back at square one, with nothing to show but a worthless degree backed by mounds of debt? Would I get stuck for another ten years in this boring town, struggling like my parents had? At least my dad had had the sense to get out, even if it was with a slut young enough to be my sister. At least he wasn't bored with life. *God, being bored must be the worst thing in the world.*

My mom knocked at the door with a smile and a plate of brownies baked special just for me. She was glad I was back. I could tell she hated this boredom as much as I did, but she felt stuck. Too old to change, too tired to change, too...something, but she had grown used to it and had learned to live with it. My homecoming had to have been the highlight of her year. Looking at her, I felt sympathy, but also fear: fear that I would become the same trapped person. And an even greater fear that I would resignedly accept it.

Taking a bite of brownie, I gazed once again out the window. Dark clouds were overtaking the sky, and it had begun to sprizzle—you know, that type of light rainfall between a sprinkle and a drizzle. As I stared at the tiny drops flinging themselves against my window, I continued to ponder my current situation. There had to be a way to break this drab cycle. It had to be within my power to change things. But was it really up to me? Did I have a choice? If so, how was I supposed to do it? The questions chased each other around my mind, just like the clouds in the gray sky outside.

The rain began to descend with increasing volume and intensity, as if to mirror my inner turmoil. The heavens grumbled and spat angrily at the earth while I sat, inches away from the turbulent weather, mulling over my unsettled present and uncertain future.

A sharp rap at the window startled me out of my reverie. Rising from my chair, I leaned forward and rubbed away some of the fog that had misted over the cool glass. There was nothing there. *Must be the rain hitting the pane,* I figured, my thoughts rhyming unconsciously.

Puzzled, I sat back in my chair. I had just opened a book when I heard the rap again, three times in succession. This was no rain striking the window. This was a persistent knocking. As I bolted from my seat in full investigation mode, another sound met my attentive ears. It sounded like…like muffled screaming.

I leaned toward the window again and placed my ear against it. Yes, there was definitely somebody screaming on the other side. I was turning to face the glass again when, suddenly, I was confronted by a pair of bulging eyes.

I leapt back with a little shriek. These eyes were enormous. I couldn't even see the head they were attached to as they filled the entire window, unblinking—two giant pupils surrounded by a sea of white. My room was plunged into semidarkness, the eyes blocking all light from the outside. Only the shimmering whites provided waves of flickering phosphorescent light that danced in menacing patterns across every surface in the room.

Time seemed to freeze as I willed myself to move. Stepping slowly toward the window, I could hear the muffled screaming again. I strained to make out words as I cautiously approached, but I couldn't hear anything intelligible.

Soon I was once again face to face with those gargantuan, motionless eyeballs. A few atoms' worth of easily breakable glass was the only thing between us. Mustering up courage, I raised my arm slowly, clenched my fist, breathed in deeply…and rapped firmly on the window.

I instantly crouched to the floor beneath the sill with a cowardly whimper, shaking with fear, half expecting those glowing eyes to crash through the glass and bear down on top of me. It was several heart-thudding seconds before I realized that the screaming had stopped. All was quiet, except for my pulse pounding in my ears. Slowly raising my head, I stole a fearful glance upward at the window.

The eyes were still there, still staring down at me, still unblinking. I panicked and pushed away from the wall, clambering backward across the floor while my eyes remained fixed in a paralytic gaze at the freakish nightmare outside. I tried yelling for Mom, but even my voice seemed too scared to leave the safety of my throat. All I could do was gape in horror and wait for whatever happened next.

And then they blinked.

Boy, did I find my voice then! Scream after scream surged from my throat as I pressed my back against the opposite wall, my legs flailing as I tried to push back even farther, my hands grasping instinctively for any projectile I could find. My fingers found a sock, which I hurled at the window, but the coward aborted its mission halfway across the room and fell limply to the carpet. The next object I thrust at the glass was an eraser; not to be outdone, it sailed over the sock and struck the window soundly with a little *boink.*

The eyes blinked again, only this time the blinking was accompanied by a loud whooshing sound, like the sound you hear if you jump on an air mattress with the valve open. I watched in disbelief as the eyeballs in the window started to shrink slowly. Cracks of light poured in around the outside as the shimmering round disks grew ever smaller by the second.

Finally I could see the head these bulbous spheres were attached to. Thick, scaly blue skin covered an oddly shaped head with a single tiny horn poking straight out the top. As the figure outside continued to shrink, other features of the face came into view: These included a hooked nose and thick lips, the latter of which were tinged a purplish hue. A narrow chin and elongated forehead rounded out the creature's face. He looked rather like a blue light bulb. But those eyes—God, those eyes! They must've taken up a good 72% of his head.

As he shrank further, I began to see more of the strange figure's body. Tiny hands attached to spindly arms grasped the sill to keep from falling, and as he finished shrinking with one final, weak *whoosh,* the creature vaulted his equally thin legs up onto the sill. He stood up and pressed his scaly blue hands against the glass, peering in at me. He took up no more space now than the average cat and consequently was far less frightening.

I stared in puzzled confusion at the odd, hairless creature. The only article of clothing he wore on his disproportionate body was a thin black belt, which only served to hold in place a miniature jet pack on his back. He was no longer screaming, but I could see his purple lips moving, as if trying to get my attention. I slowly picked myself up off the floor and stepped once again toward the window, leaning in carefully to try to ascertain what the creature was saying.

"Hey!" I heard a pinched voice cry. "Open the window, why don't you. I'm all wet, and it's cold as Mars out here!" His was an odd voice, slightly nasal with an unfamiliar accent. I shook my head at him. I wasn't about to let this thing into my bedroom.

"Oh, come on, I won't hurt you," he chuckled back. "I only flew in too big, and my lips suctioned themselves to your living room window. I mean no harm." He shot me what I assumed to be his best puppy-eyes attempt. It wasn't really working, but I was curious. Besides, I was feeling rather brave at the moment, given the size shift that had occurred.

"Look, I'll only open it a crack so I can hear you better," I called back through the glass. "Then I want you to tell me what you're doing here." The creature nodded and removed his hands from the window, allowing me to lift it slowly, just an inch. "Now, who the hell are you?"

"I'm Qarl," he said proudly, planting his legs firmly on the sill and squaring his tiny shoulders, his hands on (what I guessed were) his hips.

"Carl?"

"No. Qarl," he corrected me.

"That's what I said. Carl."

"No, I can tell you're not pronouncing the *Q*."

"How the fuck can you tell that?"

"You mean 'fuq.'"

I slammed the window. *Smartass.*

He started screaming again. *Great.* I was worried that Mom would hear…although if she hadn't heard my wretched screaming two minutes prior, she probably wasn't going to hear this thing. Regardless, I didn't want to chance it, so I flung the window open again, desperate to silence this creature and get rid of him.

"Would you shut up!" I whispered loudly at Qarl. "We have neighbors."

"Oh, you mean the lovely brown house next door?" he asked. "Very pretty indeed. Not like this dump." He picked critically at the chipping paint on the sill.

"Stop that!" I scolded him. "Look, if I let you in, will you be quiet, tell me what you're doing here, and then get the hell out?"

"Yes, yes! Just please let me in. My lips are turning blue."

After pausing one last time to give myself a chance to not regret what I was about to do, I held my breath and raised the window completely. Qarl nodded gratefully and hopped off the sill onto the bedroom floor, leaving a small puddle on the carpet in the process.

"Thank you kindly," he said cheerfully, pacing around the room and familiarizing himself with its contents as I turned and shut the window. "Cozy dwelling you have here." He picked up the book I had been reading and flipped through it, holding it upside down the whole while. Irritated, I snatched it from him.

"Enough of this. Who are you, where did you come from, how did you get stuck to my window, and why are you here?"

Qarl held up a finger as I spoke. "Hold on. I must write these questions down."

Before I could stop him, he stuck his hand out and tore a page out of the book I was holding. Reaching up to his head, he plucked his little horn off and began using it as a pencil, scribbling rapidly from right to left on the margins of the page.

"Ok, first question: who am I?" he began. "Well, like I said before, I am Qarl." He paused a moment and stared at me, as if to let the *Q* sink in better or something. "Where am I from? Well, that's a tricky question. I've lived all over the place, but my current residence is on the planet X@X—someone like you would pronounce it as 'Zax,' I suppose." Here he shook his head, likely considering me quite stupid, before returning his gaze to his reference sheet. "How did I get here? Well, I parked my teletransportube behind that rusty statue over there." He pointed out the window at the water tower. "I then launched myself over here…but I overestimated the size of your dwelling and had set my body coordinates too large. As I went to land here, my lips suctioned themselves to your downstairs window, and I was just dangling there when I realized that I could reach your bedroom window. I grabbed the sill, pulled myself up as far as my lips would stretch, peeked in, and there you were!"

Qarl had been pacing in ever-quickening circles as he answered my list of questions, speaking faster and faster before finishing his last sentence with a triumphant wave of his "pencil." I understood less than half of what he had just said, but that didn't matter to me at the moment.

"So that leaves just one question, then," I said. "And I think it's the most important one, so if you screw around with me, I'll just chuck you right back out the window."

A flicker of fear crossed Qarl's face as I leaned in closer.

"Why are you here?"

Chapter B

Motioning for me to sit down, Qarl replaced his horn on his head and took on a serious expression. Clearly, his answer to my question was important and required my full attention.

Well, he had it. I plopped down on the floor and leaned forward curiously.

"You must come with me," Qarl began earnestly. "X@X needs your help. They're going to get rid of us, They are. They don't even care anymore."

I was confused. "You mean the planet? Who's getting rid of you? Who doesn't care? I don't understand."

"I don't have much time to explain. I've been sent by the Queen to summon you. I'm to take you back to X@X in my teletransportube tonight. I'll explain more on the way."

"Wait, what queen? What are you talking about?" Qarl wasn't making any sense.

"You'll see when you get there. You must come with me," he repeated, tugging on my sleeve.

"Whoa, whoa, whoa. I'm not going anywhere with you, dude," I said, standing up. "You're crazy."

I began to walk toward the door, thoroughly done with this guy. But Qarl was quicker. He scuttled across the room and placed himself between me and the door.

"You don't understand," he said, his voice dropping to a whisper. "I have…candy."

I stopped. This new piece of information was very tempting indeed. It certainly changed things. My mouth began to water as my sugar addiction stirred deep within me. However, I had to be certain. This was a serious matter.

Stepping forward, I raised one eyebrow. "What kind of candy?"

Qarl motioned me closer. I leaned down with anticipation. In a furtive whisper, he revealed,

"Milky Ways."

Ah! The best kind! Why hadn't he said so sooner? This stranger sure knew how to bargain. Now, my mom had always taught me never to go with strangers under any circumstances. But this one had candy. That was different. My decision was made.

"I'm in!"

π π π π π

The moon was full. The clouds had long vanished, along with the rain. A chilly breeze rocked the trees with a heavy sigh. Up ahead, the water tower creaked a welcome. We were almost there.

I had found it odd that Mom was nowhere to be seen when Qarl and I crept downstairs and out the front door. However, I had too many things on my mind (and too much candy in my mouth) to give it a second thought.

Qarl and I had quickly crossed the street, raced across the parking lot, and sneaked around the store and through the yards beyond. We were now standing before the rusty old excuse of a water tower. It looked huge up close; I had forgotten how big it was. I had tried to climb it a few times as a kid, but a couple tetanus shots had cured me of that. And now here I was, standing once more beneath it, slightly in awe that it was just as large to me now as it had seemed so many years before.

Qarl bowed slightly, as if perhaps this thing were a deity of ours. I smirked and pushed past him into the trees beyond. I had only gone a few feet, however, when I stopped once again. There, in a clearing ahead, sat the oddest thing ever.

A long gray metal tube rested in the darkness on the grass in front of me. It was about fifty feet in length and at least three times my height. The large craft was perfectly cylindrical, and a row of soft lights wrapped around the entire length, dimly illuminating the dark clearing.

Walking slowly from one end of the tube to the other, I noticed rockets housed in one extremity, while the opposite end narrowed to a pencil-thin point. The curved top portion of the vessel consisted of a large transparent hatch, which connected seamlessly to sets of windows along the sides of the tube and a sloping windshield in the front. A series of landing gears on the bottom kept the machine from rolling.

I reached up and touched the shiny, cold metal while Qarl stood off to the side, grinning proudly.

"This, my friend," he said, "is the Ken.10, my brand-new teletransportube. Absolute top of the line, this is. The Queen just upgraded me from a Kate.8. That thing was in bad shape."

I nodded, speechless, while I continued stroking the ship as if it were a sick dog.

"Comes with loads of new features," Qarl continued. "Reversible rockets, an updated telepod with new coordinates preloaded, the latest SimuGrav™ technology installed, a diffuser—"

"What's SimuGrav™?" I interrupted.

"It's a gravity simulator. One touch of a button in Space and weightlessness is no longer an issue."

I nodded and continued circling the ship, pausing from time to time to touch something new. It's a wonder I didn't swallow any bugs, my mouth was hanging so low. After another two minutes of this, Qarl stepped forward.

"Well? You ready to hop in? We're already behind schedule."

"Um…sure," I replied. "But how do you get—"

Qarl snapped his fingers. With a loud hiss, a ladder sprang out of a recessed compartment on the side of the spacecraft. Unfolding itself smoothly, it stretched out to the ground in front of me with a pneumatic sigh. Qarl hopped past me and up the ladder, three rungs at a time. I followed cautiously.

As I climbed, I began to see inside the massive ship. Rows of buttons, dials, switches, gauges, levers, wheels, pedals, cranks, screens, and lights littered the interior. Two quite comfy-looking chairs were situated toward the front, while a small metal pod sat in the back.

At the top of the ladder, Qarl snapped his fingers again, and, this time, two sections of the transparent hatch popped open. Lights began blinking, and a soft, purring sound arose from the bowels of the vessel. Qarl turned to me, smiling.

"SimuShush™ noise reduction technology," he said proudly, referring to the whisper-quiet engine. He motioned with his hand to one of the hatches. "Hop in!"

Stepping over the top rung, I dropped into the tube and glanced around. The entire interior was padded with a carpetlike material. Mirrors scattered throughout the ship afforded a view of every inch of the vessel, inside and out. The abundance of reflections made the machine feel much more spacious on the inside than it had looked from the outside.

I selected a chair and sat down. Damn, was this thing comfy! It swiveled, reclined, and rocked in every conceivable way you could wish. Padding and cushions as soft as can be made me feel as if I were sitting in God's lap. Each chair was also anchored to a track that spanned the entire length of the tube so that one could slide from screen to lever to dial and back with fluid ease.

Qarl removed his jet pack and stowed it carefully underneath the front dashboard. He took his seat, punched a few buttons, and slid over to me. "Are you ready?" he asked with a wink.

I nodded. Snapping his fingers to close the hatches, Qarl gripped the wheel in front of him. "Here we go!" he shouted excitedly, pulling back hard with both hands.

Without hesitation, the pointed end of the ship began rising slowly into the air, pivoting on one of the rear landing gears. As we tilted backward, our chairs rotated themselves so that we stayed upright at all times. Every screen and dial reoriented itself to match Qarl's position as the tube slowly reached a vertical position with astounding smoothness.

Once the rockets faced the ground squarely and the needle nose was aimed for the stars, Qarl punched the floor pedal. I was thrown back in my chair as we hurtled into the sky, the trees dropping away as though we were in the fastest elevator imaginable.

The lights in the neighboring towns came into view and just as quickly faded away as we rose at an alarming speed. Town after town, city after city, county after county came and went, blurring themselves under us as the earth's horizon began to look less flat and more round.

I tore my gaze away from the outside and looked over at Qarl. His huge eyes were even huger, and a grin stretched across his blue face. Clearly, he loved the Ken.10.

I smiled and returned my focus to the black outdoors. The only lights I could see now were the twinkling stars, which seemed to grow clearer, brighter, and more numerous as we continued to soar higher and higher.

After an exhilarating few minutes, Qarl began to slow the craft down. Gradually the nose lowered and the interior adjusted itself until front and back were level once again. Qarl maneuvered the craft carefully into orbital position and began circling the earth.

"I want you to enjoy the view," he said and, with a flick of a switch, cut the engines.

All was silent. The craft orbited without a sound…falling freely…weightless. I felt myself rise out of my chair and move toward the glass. Only a thin transparent layer separated me from space, emptiness, nothingness.

The earth looked beautiful from here, a giant marble swirling with rich colors and detail. In that moment, I found it hard to comprehend that I lived on that floating ball. All of those people in all of those massive crowded cities…we were all just small and alone really, drifting through depths of infinite blackness. Staring at my planet from this point of view altered my perspective rather quickly.

The earth wasn't the only eye-catcher in the dark sky that night, however. Off to the side, the moon loomed larger than I had ever seen it, catching the sun's rays along its pits and craters and reflecting them dutifully back to the earth. It was all so breathtakingly beautiful.

Qarl hit the SimuGrav™ button, and I settled back into my chair. "Nice, huh?" he said happily.

"You can say that again," I managed to whisper. My own voice sounded so loud compared to the magnificent stillness.

"Well," Qarl continued, "I hate to cut the party short, but we're running low on time and fuel. Besides, I have to make a quick stop on the Moon before we head back to X@X." He restarted the engines with a snap and began steering the ship out of orbit.

"The moon?" I asked. "What for?"

"I have to feed the Man in the Moon," he replied matter-of-factly. I laughed out loud. This was too funny. Qarl launched a glare in my direction.

"Wait—you're serious?" I asked, puzzled.

"Of course I'm serious!" he retorted. I could tell he was slightly offended. "The Queen wanted me to do it on my way back. She usually gets Zaaq to do it, but seeing as I was going to be in the area, she ordered me to."

I was more than a bit taken aback and still not quite sure he was serious. "Um, so what does he eat?" I asked, a grin playing at the corners of my lips.

"Well, he usually prefers asteroid chunks. Also, chicken. Let's see, what else?"

"Green cheese?" I ventured, smiling.

Qarl was not amused. "What are you, five? Green cheese!" He shook his head incredulously. Obviously, I was stupid for thinking that the man in the moon would consider such a ludicrous diet choice. I sat back in my chair, slightly flabbergasted, unsure of what to think of this conversation anymore.

"He also is partial to a good mustard & tomato sandwich," Qarl continued. "But the Queen's got him on a diet now." He held up a large cylindrical container and shook it. "Nebula shakes," he said with a grin. I shook my head in bemused disbelief. Qarl was definitely not pulling my leg.

Resuming my gaze out the windows, I was surprised to see a few small pellets *plink* against the side. "Space debris," I heard Qarl mutter as he swerved to avoid the larger pieces. The flying detritus hitting the glass reminded me of something I had been meaning to ask.

"Say, Qarl, how did you shrink when you were stuck up against my window back home and I was throwing things at you?"

Qarl reached into one of his skin folds and held out his hand. He was holding the eraser I had thrown at the bedroom window.

"This," he said, handing it to me. "I took the liberty of grabbing it on our way out, just in case."

"In case of what?" I asked, curious.

"In case I need to shrink again in an emergency. It's very small and convenient," he replied. I wasn't quite following. As if sensing that, Qarl pointed at the eraser in my hand. "Rubber. Rubber is what makes me shrink…when it's thrown at me, that is."

"How come it has to be thrown at you? And why rubber?" I asked. I turned the tiny eraser over in my hand, slightly intrigued by this new discovery about an everyday household item I took for granted.

"Well, technically, most firm objects thrown at me will cause me to shrink. You see, my skin is extremely elastic. It can stretch to great proportions and shrink to equally small proportions under the right conditions. When a hard object strikes my skin at a particular velocity threshold, the applied force makes the fibers in my skin contract sharply, causing me to shrink in direct proportion to the force with which the object hits me. I've found rubber to be the best material since its bouncy nature produces a very short, focused point of pressure when it comes in contact with my skin."

"So then what do you use to grow?" I asked.

"Cotton," he replied, pointing at my shirt. "Or any equally soft material. Similar principle: the soft fabric rubbing on my skin stimulates the fibers and causes them to expand, also in direct proportion to how vigorously the material is rubbed against my skin."

Qarl gestured to a large helmet sitting on the dash. Two flexible arms protruded from the sides. "That right there is my size adjuster. It's an expandable helmet I've designed so that I can adjust my size without trial and error. One arm contains rubber and the other, cotton. I put on the helmet, set the dial, and voilà! I get punched or rubbed until I'm the right size.

"Which reminds me," he continued, picking up the helmet and placing it on his head, "your eraser shrunk me way too small. I need to grow to a more comfortable size."

With that, he rotated the dial, and the cotton arm came whirring to life, rubbing his skin gently in circular motions. I watched in amazement as Qarl slowly began to grow before my eyes. His appendages extended, his torso stretched, and his massive head grew even more prodigious. The whole while, he continued to pilot the craft skillfully, as if indifferent to the transformation taking place to his body.

By the time Qarl removed the helmet and replaced it on the dash, he had grown to about waist height. I was fascinated by what I had just witnessed but still had a question about the whole shrinkage and growth process.

"I'm a bit confused," I said. "I never actually hit you with the eraser. It hit the window, remember?"

"Yes, but I was in contact with the window at the time," Qarl replied. "The rubber striking it sent shockwaves at the appropriate frequency through the glass and into my skin."

I nodded, finally understanding. Still fingering the eraser, I briefly contemplated chucking it at him to see the effect, but something outside the rear of the craft caught my eye.

One of the many points of light in the sky seemed to be growing steadily larger. Stuffing the eraser into my pocket, I slid my chair to the rear of the ship and peered into the darkness. Amid the bright white dots that I knew were stars, a soft, pulsating blue sphere of light stood out larger than the rest. It seemed to grow bigger and brighter and bluer with every second.

Something wasn't right.

"Um, Qarl?" I called to the front. "You might want to take a look."

Qarl turned around, a slightly annoyed expression on his face, as if he thought that I had another stupid "touristy" question. I gestured to the ball of light, which had become quite large by that point.

A shadow crossed Qarl's face. He whirled and punched the foot pedal, gripping the wheel tightly as we surged forward. I was almost thrown out of my chair.

"What's going on?" I yelled.

"Rogue comet!" he hollered back. "It's Them, I know it!"

He jerked the wheel back and forth, and the tube lurched from side to side in response. I opened my mouth to ask who he was talking about, but a quick glance back out the window showed me that there were more pressing matters at hand.

The glowing blue ball of swirling gases and ice was bearing down on us fast. I gasped at how close it was. Qarl swung the ship back and forth, up and down, but the comet stayed locked on our tail, speeding closer and closer.

"It's no use!" Qarl shouted. "It's one of Theirs, and it's honed in on us. We can't shake it."

"Can't you put up a force shield or something?" I hollered back, my mind scrambling through years of science-fiction movies for plausible solutions to this problem.

"This teletransportube model doesn't come with a SimuShield™," Qarl wailed. He turned to me. "You'll have to take the controls."

"*What!?!*" I exclaimed. "Are you nuts?"

"I have to use the diffuser in the back. You'll have to control the ship while I do. There's no other option."

"No, wait!" I started to shout, but it was too late. With one swift motion, Qarl shoved back from the controls and slid to the back where I was.

"Go!" he yelled. "I'll operate the diffuser. Just take the wheel." He gave my chair a forceful push.

I turned to protest once more, but the blinding blue light almost upon us changed my tune. Spurred into action, I rushed to the front of the craft. Gripping the wheel tightly, I called back to Qarl. He had removed a panel on the back wall and was pressing buttons furiously.

"What if I hit something?" I hollered nervously.

"Relax!" Qarl shot back. "You won't hit anything. Besides, anything big enough to cause damage you'd see coming from miles away. Plenty of time to avoid it."

Unless it's another comet, I thought grimly.

"So what do I do?" I shouted as I clutched the wheel, my hands sweating profusely.

"We can't risk leading this comet into the Moon. Aim the ship toward Aries."

"Toward what?"

"ARIES!" Qarl shouted. "The constellation."

"Where the hell is Aries?" I yelled, looking back and forth out each window in a frenzied panic. I didn't even remember what Aries was supposed to resemble.

"Use the compass!"

Compass? What compass? I scanned the dash frantically. To my right was a dial with a swinging needle. Oddly, my first reaction was surprise at how out of place a simple mechanical device like this looked in such a digital environment. Instead of any directional markings I was familiar with, the gauge was marked with the constellations of the zodiac: Aquarius, Pisces, Leo, Scorpius, Ophiuchus, Aries—there it was!

I yanked the wheel hard to the left, and the ship obeyed with a groan. I watched the needle closely; as soon as it hovered above the Aries demarcation, I corrected the wheel, and we leveled out.

Glancing in the rear-facing mirror, I saw the comet roar once again into view, our little detour scarcely affecting its mission. My heart caught in my throat. The image of the monster almost swallowed the entire mirror, and a loud rushing sound began to fill the cabin, growing more and more intense with each minute—no, second. Even worse, I hadn't heard from Qarl in a while.

"Qarl?" I called back over my shoulder, my shaking voice betraying my terror. "You about ready with that diffu—"

The entire cabin was suddenly bathed in a harsh red light. A low-pitched humming sound pulsated through the tube from one end to the other and back again, drowning out the comet's roar. Whirling around in my chair, I saw Qarl silhouetted against the glow, his hands grasping a joystick. A bright, red laser beamed outwards from a device mounted on the rear exterior of the spaceship, fanning out into a cone shape and surrounding the comet's fierce glow. Roar and hum fought a fierce battle as the red light grew more intense. The cabin began to shake violently.

For a tense eternity of seconds, Qarl and I watched, frozen in awe and fear. The blue light slowly began to shrink in size while still approaching closer and closer. I braced myself against the dash and squinted as the noises and lights grew more intense. I didn't even realize at the moment that my hands had slipped from the wheel.

"It's breaking up!" Qarl shouted, an edge of strained excitement to his voice. Blue seemed to grow brighter and roar louder even as it shrank, as if it were defiantly refusing to die. Red hummed intensely in response, enveloping the enemy unrelentingly.

Then, without warning, both lights vanished from the sky, and their accompanying sounds disappeared without an echo. For a fraction of a second, all was black and silent…and then, the loudest and brightest explosion I had ever felt or witnessed swept over the ship, sending massive shockwaves along the entire length and flinging the tube forward with a dramatic jolt. I was pitched out of my chair headfirst and tumbled to the floor. On my back facing the transparent ceiling, I saw dense clouds of dust, ice, and debris race past, some pelting our ship like hail on a tin roof.

A shadow leapt over me: it was Qarl. He raced to the dash and grabbed the wheel to steady the rocking tube. Mashing the accelerator and pulling up on the wheel, he maneuvered the ship up and away from the debris field, leaving the torrent of broken-up comet pieces to soar unhindered through space below us. Soon the moon was once again in our sights.

After scrambling to my feet and brushing myself off, I resumed my seat, unsure if I dared to let out a relieved sigh. Still stunned by the close call, I sat in silence, trying to process what had just happened. As if anticipating my thoughts, Qarl spoke.

"I don't have time to explain everything right now. We'll be landing on the Moon in about 1,900 mirkrons." He paused and glanced over at me. "10 minutes your time," he clarified.

I nodded wordlessly as Qarl skillfully brought the ship in until we were skimming over the moon's rocky, pitted surface. He guided the tube to a flat, smooth area and touched down like a plane would have, with barely a bump.

"I won't take long. You just stay here," he instructed as the tube rolled to a stop. With a snap of his fingers, he shut the engines off. Moving quickly, he wasted no time in cramming several of the nebula shakes into a knapsack, slinging the bag over his shoulder, and heading for the hatch.

"Feeding time," he said with a wink. With that, he flung open the hatch and hopped over the side, but not before grabbing a gun off a rack and stuffing it hurriedly into his belt. I rose and peered out of the hatch after him, watching him cross the dusty terrain as fast as his little legs would carry him, until he disappeared over a hill and into a crater.

I dropped back into the tube and looked around. All was quiet and still.

I was alone.

Chapter C

The quiet was slightly chilling. I tried not to let the thought sink in that I was alone, all by myself, not miles away from home, but *miles* away from home. I wondered what my mom was doing at the moment. Had she discovered my absence? Was she worrying about me? What if she freaked out and decided to call the cops? Shaking my head, I resolved not to let my mind wander to things I had no control over. To keep myself occupied, I decided to explore the inside of the tube.

I chose to start at the back. The first gadget I inspected was the diffuser panel Qarl had used to destroy the comet. I grasped the joystick cautiously and pretended I was blasting other celestial bodies out of the sky. I rather wished I owned a cool spaceship like this.

It wasn't long before my attention turned to the metal pod in the corner. I had been curious as to its function since I first stepped onto the craft. It was cylindrical in shape and large enough to hold a man, maybe two. I looked around for a door or hatch, but while I could see where several openings were outlined in the cold metal, they were sealed shut with no handles to open them.

Curious, I tried snapping my fingers as I had seen Qarl do. Nothing happened. I pressed on edges and corners, looking for a secret panel or button that would allow me access to this curious device.

Nothing.

Frowning with disappointment, I finally abandoned the effort and focused my attention to the rest of the ship. Not much was housed along the midsection except for some screens and mirrors. The front, however, was a treasure trove of technology.

The Ken.10 had an impressive dashboard filled with gadgets from a nerd's wet dream. I didn't know what most of these gauges and levers did, but the blinking colored lights were mesmerizing. Large screens mounted into the walls displayed various data: current location, weather patterns, star coordinates. A few gauges off to the side presented air pressure, temperature, and atmospheric readings.

I began to peruse the contents of Qarl's cluttered dash. There was the compass I had used earlier. Also, Qarl's size-adjuster helmet. I picked it up and placed it on my head with a grin. Such an odd yet clever gadget. But it made sense: Qarl was indeed an odd yet clever alien. I wondered what his day-to-day life was like on this planet X@X he called home. Perhaps he would show me once our mission was complete, whatever it was.

My mind began to fill with questions that the adventures of the evening had previously held back. *Why was I summoned so hurriedly from Earth? Who is this queen I'm supposed to meet? Why is my presence so urgently necessary? What if this is all a trap and I'm actually in danger?* Once again, I shook my head to clear it, choosing not to worry about conundrums I could not resolve at the moment.

I turned my attention back to exploring the Ken.10. So many interesting contrivances littered the inside of Qarl's ship, most of them quite high-tech. But something different made me do a double take.

Standing out rather oddly from all the digital, technological equipment, a small dog-eared manual caught my eye. It was tucked into a corner on a small shelf above the dash. I removed the helmet from my head and reached for the wrinkled booklet. Pulling it from its shelf, I glanced at the title: *The Advice Manual.*

Strange, I thought, opening it and flipping through the pages. Most of them were blank, while a few held inconsequential scribbles. I stopped on a circled page: page 118. At the top was written a single word: "Here." Scanning down the page, off to the side I noticed doodles of what looked like branches, red and snaking down the margins. Right beside the branches were tiny sketches of locks. Yielding to my increasing curiosity, my eyes followed the words written in tiny print at the bottom. Advice it definitely was, keys to life and wisdom apparently.

Everything. Take everything in life as a lesson. Hold on to every moment as a sign. Aspire to laugh, take time to choose, ponder every detail you leave behind. All are true and truly clues.

Glancing at the very bottom of the page, equations and symbols and random numbers caught my eye, 72 being the number predominantly written among a slew of various addition calculations cluttering the margin around the page number. Ending the page was a directive to continue reading.

I flipped through the rest of the manual, but the remaining pages were blank. *What an odd book,* I thought. With a shrug, I closed the manual and replaced it on the shelf.

I slouched back in my chair and swiveled aimlessly back and forth. I wished Qarl would return soon; I wasn't very comfortable being left alone on a desolate moon. To be honest, I wasn't really comfortable either with the thought that my only hope for survival or safe return home rested with a little blue alien I had just met. But that was indeed where I found myself, and I wasn't going to let panic or fear overtake me.

A large red button on the steering wheel in front of me captured my notice. It was situated in the center, right where a horn would be on its automobile counterpart. Leaning forward, I pressed it.

Hooooooooonk!

I jumped at the loud noise. Glancing sheepishly out the window, I hoped Qarl hadn't heard it. What would he need a horn in space for anyway? I smiled to myself as I imagined Qarl stuck in some sort of intergalactic traffic jam, honking his way around other spaceships, growing frustrated with every passing mirkron.

Where *was* he?

I stood up and peered out one of the windows, trying to catch a glimpse of him trotting back to the tube. All I could see was the moon's gray, shadow-filled surface, the immense blackness above it, and the tiny white points of starlight hovering in place.

Off to one side, right where the moon's shadowy horizon blurred with the blackness of space, I noticed a pair of yellow stars. These didn't quite shine like the rest. I tried to think back to my science classes in high school. Didn't the color of the light relate to the temperature of the star? Or was it the distance? I couldn't remember as I stared more intently at the odd stellar pair.

And then they moved.

My heart skipped a beat. Was I imagining things? *Stars don't move like that,* I thought. The yellow pair shifted again.

A shiver went through my body as I realized that these weren't celestial bodies.

They were eyes.

As I watched, frozen in fear, the yellow lights slowly emerged from the shadows. The body they were attached to was even more frightening than the menacing eyes themselves. A slimy gray form crawling on all fours crept from the blackness. It was grotesque in appearance and size and had a spiked tail that it swung threateningly. Its long, groping fingers clawed at the dust as it approached, while its dead, yellow eyes stared up at me. A wicked grin stretched across its wrinkled face, as if it relished my fear.

The creature continued to approach the ship. Light bounced off fangs that dripped with thick saliva. A guttural snarl emerged from the belly of the beast, traveling through the sealed hatch and making the hairs on my neck stand on end. Trembling, I was beginning to back away from the window when the night horizon once again caught my eye.

There were more yellow stars. Dozens of them. Pair after pair of glowing eyes. I froze, hoping that I was only imagining things. I did not have to wonder long. As if on cue, a quivering horde of these creatures swept from the shadows en masse, clawing its way toward the ship from all sides. Countless vacant eyes stared right through me, and every mouth stretched itself into an evil smile.

I whirled around and ran to the back of the tube, searching frantically for a weapon or an emergency lever or something. Where the hell was Qarl? My search was turning up nothing.

Suddenly, I heard a thud against the side of the tube, followed by a low growl and intense scratching. I dropped to the floor and crawled as fast as I could back to the front of the ship. Pinning myself against the side, I slowly raised my head and peered out the window—and came face to face with a pair of glowing eyes and a snarling grin. I ducked in terror. They had already reached the ship.

I could hear the spine-tingling scratches as the little monsters groped for a way into the cabin. I slid across the floor and into the shadows underneath the dash. The sounds of the creatures growling, trying to find a way in, sent shivers through my very bones. This was it. *I'm going to die here,* I thought in panic.

A loud *thunk* tore my attention upward. One of the beasts had found its way onto the transparent hatch directly above where I crouched, hiding. Its terrifying eyes stared down at me as its bony fingers fumbled for a way in. My heart drummed rapidly in my chest, and sweat poured down my face. My mouth went dry as I could taste the fear coursing through my body. *Death by comet would've been so much more merciful,* I thought regretfully.

Just then, a piercing, high-pitched sound struck my ears. I instinctively clapped my hands against them to shut out the noise. Still glancing upward, I saw the creature recoil and begin to convulse wildly. Turning, it leapt off the hatch with a primal screech. The scratching and growls ceased from all sides, being replaced with wounded squeals.

With my hands still pressed firmly on my ears against the strident sound, I wriggled out from my hiding place. Shuffling to one of the windows, I dared to steal a glance out.

What I saw was completely unexpected.

On a large moon rock in the distance, Qarl stood poised, his feet apart and his skinny arms grasping the gun he had taken with him earlier. It seemed to be the source of the awful sound. With a determined look in his giant eyes, he swept it from side to side, aiming it at the creatures, who were now scrambling fervently to get away from the horrid, unending noise. Each beast caught in direct line with the beam of sound recoiled with a pained yelp and fell to the ground, writhing.

Qarl began to move forward slowly, still sweeping his gun back and forth. The creatures—suffering as they were—were relentless, however. Once the gun was no longer directed at them, they rose and continued skulking toward the ship, like a stubborn child bent on possessing a certain toy, regardless of the consequences.

Qarl continued making his way back to the tube, turning and sweeping constantly, keeping the beasts momentarily at bay. When he was a few feet from the ship, he caught my eye and motioned for me to open the hatch. I complied, wincing slightly as I had to remove my hands from my ears to perform the task. As soon as the hatch was open, Qarl shut off the gun, turned, and, with a running jump, leapt into the tube. I quickly shut the hatch after him.

I was not a moment too soon. The instant the sound ceased, the monsters surged toward the spaceship once again. Qarl reached up and locked the hatch as the creatures swarmed over the tube, scratching and clawing and growling and screeching. A few grabbed moon rocks and began pelting our craft, desperately trying to breach the exterior.

Qarl rushed to the dash. Adjusting a few dials, he snapped his fingers to start the engines. Nothing. He looked up, surprised, and snapped them again. Still nothing. Bending over the dash, he furiously pressed a few buttons, but the engines did not respond. An error message beeped on one of the many screens. Qarl squinted to read it.

"Blast it!" he exclaimed, punching the dash. "They've jammed all the engines with rocks. We'll never be able to fly out of here now."

This wasn't news I wanted to hear.

"Wait, we can't fly out of here?" I repeated, my voice rising in growing panic. "What are we going to do?"

"There's only one thing to do," Qarl responded. "We'll have to…leave the ship behind." He said this with a twinge of regret in his voice, as if this was one of the hardest decisions he had ever had to make.

"WHAT!?!" I exclaimed. "Are you insane? We can't go out there. We'll be kil—"

Qarl grabbed my arm, pulling me to the back of the ship with him. "Come on!" he ordered.

We stopped in front of the large metal pod that I had attempted exploring before. Qarl clapped twice, and a panel popped open with a hiss. *So that's how you open it.*

The interior of the pod was padded but was essentially as bland and minimalistic as the exterior. On the other side of the open panel was a row of dials, knobs, and buttons, along with a small screen. Qarl fumbled with a few of the dials.

Meanwhile, outside the tube, the noises were getting louder and louder. Every inch of the ship's outer shell was crawling with the bloodthirsty beasts. I shivered.

A slight whirring sound brought me back to the task at hand. Lights on the panel and inside the pod began blinking. Qarl had succeeded in whatever it was he had been attempting.

"This is my telepod," he explained hurriedly. "It will teleport us to X@X." He pointed to the miniature screen.

"See? I've pulled up the coordinates for the main telepod located on X@X. Once we get in and I press this button, we'll be teleported straight there. Now, get in."

I hesitated. Flying around space in a tube was one thing, but everybody knew that teleportation didn't exist. I wasn't sure I wanted to be trapped in a metal pod, subject to the whims of a loony alien's "scientific" experiments. Who knew what this pod could do once buttons were pressed?

I opened my mouth to object, but a loud crash made me whirl around. One of the creatures had successfully broken one of the hatches with a rock and was now dropping into the cabin with a triumphant screech. Its buddies converged on the hole, each eagerly awaiting its turn to descend into the conquered tube. Qarl turned and gave me a shove.

"Go, go, go! Get in!" he shouted. I tumbled through the narrow opening and fell to the padded floor of the telepod. Turning back to the panel, I saw Qarl give one last wistful look around his spaceship before leaping through the doorway after me. He clapped his hands to shut the panel, just before one of the beasts slammed into the metal side. With one swift motion, Qarl reached up and mashed the big green button on the door.

Whooooooooooooooooooosh!

The instant the button was depressed, everything went dark. I felt my surroundings begin to spin around me, while, somehow, I remained stationary. A loud, pulsing roar met my ears and surged through my entire being, growing more intense by the second.

Then, in a flash, I felt myself being sucked into space and time, while at the same instant being pulled away from it. I was everywhere and nowhere all at once. I felt intense pressure and yet nothingness. Everything was black and silent, yet I was acutely aware of noise and light all around me. Blurred moments whizzed past me with astounding clarity. It was as if the fabric of the universe itself was swirling around me, in me, and through me.

I could feel colors, smell sounds, taste emotions, see thoughts, hear light, sense reality—it was all so surreal. It felt as if all the questions that I had ever asked in my life were being answered at an alarming speed and being replaced with new questions. Life and the universe at once made perfect sense and no sense. I was still, spinning, motionless, tumbling, happy, sad, laughing, angry, tranquil, afraid, inside my body, outside my body, and any other pair of random opposites that I can use to show you what a truly indescribable experience it was.

(The only thing that I can really remember with certainty from the trip is that the colors of the rainbow combined with the chromatic music scale somehow explain all the unanswered questions of math and science. Don't ask me why or how; that's just what I recall.)

With one final *whoosh* and a slurp to top it off, everything suddenly stabilized and brightened. I saw the ground zoom in as if I were being dropped from ten feet up. I hit the padded floor hard, temporarily knocking the wind out of me. Beside me, Qarl flopped unceremoniously on his bulbous head. Brushing himself off, he stood up almost immediately. Clearly, he had done this before and was rather used to it.

With a groan, I rolled over and slowly looked around. We were still in a pod, only this one was a lot larger. I staggered to my feet, hugging the curved wall for support and feeling more than a little dizzy. Qarl had marched over to the panel and was squinting at some dials.

"What the hell were those creatures?" I asked, their terrifying images still burned into my mind.

"Those," Qarl replied matter-of-factly, tapping a few buttons, "were the Vielkrad. Some call them Moon-people, although they are not Human. Cranky bunch, aren't they…" His voice trailed off as he adjusted a few knobs.

"Wait. There are moon people?" I repeated, incredulous. "As in, they live there all the time?" I couldn't believe that horrid beasts like that inhabited our very own moon, and no one on Earth had ever known it.

"Yes, there are Moon-people," Qarl replied, his voice betraying exasperation. "But we don't talk to them."

"Who's 'we'?"

"Practically the entire galaxy. Your astronauts know about them too," he continued, as if reading my thoughts. "Why do you think they stopped sending Men to the Moon after 1972? One too many close calls with these friendly guys."

He cocked his head, pausing to read a dial before continuing. "They're an ill-mannered bunch, these Vielkrad…although not what you would call purely evil. They generally stay on the dark side and only attack when they feel their territory is threatened."

I shook my head in disbelief. "Wait, wait, wait. You mean you knew all along about these monsters living on the moon and just left me alone without warning me first?" Now I was starting to get agitated. "I could have been killed!"

"Ok, look." Qarl turned around to face me. "You would have been perfectly safe. They never would have known we were there if you hadn't blown that stupid horn. That was what alerted them, you know."

I took a step back. "Whoa, you're actually trying to blame *me* now? I'm supposed to take the blame for a danger I didn't even know existed? Besides, you never told me that I couldn't touch anything."

"That's a given!" Qarl exclaimed, his voice rising a bit. "You don't touch things you don't know about. Did I come into your house and just start touching things?"

"Actually, you did."

Qarl folded his lanky arms defiantly. "That's—neither here nor there," he huffed. "You shouldn't have been messing around with my equipment."

"And *you* should've warned me about what was out there instead of grabbing a gun for your own protection and running off."

"Hey!" Qarl jabbed a finger in my face. "I saved your life too! And what do I get in return? My beloved Ken.10 is abandoned, all alone, left to the whims of a bunch of dirty miscreants! All that beautiful, beautiful equipment lost and left to rust on your stupid Moon. I'll probably never see it again. All because of you!" His voice rose with every sentence until he was practically screeching.

"You left me *and* your precious ship with no protection!" I shouted back.

"Try not honking the horn when you don't know what's out there," he retorted, rolling his large eyes.

"You should have warned me," I repeated. "Besides, I thought sound wasn't supposed to travel in space."

"HA! Shows how much *you* know," he spat back. "You know, this is so typical of you. You grasp nothing about how stuff works in the Universe. You thought the Moon was made of green cheese."

"Oh, so *that's* stupid, but feeding a freakin' man in the moon isn't? I can't joke about green cheese, but I'm supposed to believe without question in 'rogue comets' and 'moon people'?"

Qarl stood on his tiptoes and began poking his finger earnestly in my face. "Aha! That's another thing! You don't even properly capitalize and hyphenate words like 'Moon-people' when you talk."

"How the fuck can you even tell that!?!" I yelled, thoroughly exasperated.

"You mean 'fuq,' of course. Stupid Human," he muttered.

I threw up my hands. "Enough!" I shouted. "I'm sick of being at the mercy of some stupid, cocky little blue alien that thinks he knows everything."

"Oh yeah?" Qarl shot back. "Well *I'm* sick of having to cart around a nervous, good-for-nothing Human—who can't seem to understand the most basic aspects of the Universe—just because the Queen said so."

I was seething mad now but desperately trying to keep a lid on it. "Shut up, Qarl," I warned. "Just shut up!"

Qarl did not shut up.

"And another thing!" he screamed at the top of his lungs, his blue face turning purple with out-of-control rage. "Your mom is so nebulous that they had to send a snorgon to quomple her!!!"

Now this was too far. Qarl had crossed a line. I normally do not resort to violence, but this was too much…so I hauled off and smacked him in the face.

His head fell off. I hadn't expected that.

It took me a few moments for my raging mind to fully process what had just happened: the rolling head, the twitching body, the odd lack of blood or any other kind of bodily fluid—it was all a shock to my brain. Everything slowed.

After what seemed like more-time-than-what-actually-transpired, Qarl's misshapen head finally rolled to a stop, and an awkward silence permeated the interior of the pod. I was too stricken with utter amazement to speak, and Qarl—well, he couldn't really say anything at the moment.

Had I killed him? I was scared to find out. I stepped timidly toward the head resting against the pod wall. Rather selfishly, my first thought involved how I was going to get out of there and back home if Qarl indeed was dead. The obligatory guilt wasn't far behind, however. I felt truly awful, but I hadn't meant to hit him hard. I was just trying to shut his big purple mouth.

I had just stepped gingerly over Qarl's limp body flopped on the floor in front of me when one of his hands reached up and grasped my leg. I yelped and jumped back. The headless body was animated now, legs kicking and arms flailing, trying to grab at something. I backed against the pod wall, more than a little weirded out.

Across from me, Qarl's head slowly rotated away from the wall until its eyes were staring directly at me, menacing and unblinking. In the middle of the pod, his body's hands had finally found the floor and were pushing against it, succeeding in dragging the body slowly across the floor toward me, guided by the eyes watching behind it.

As soon as the headless body was close enough to touch my shoes, I jumped over it to the other side of the pod. Reaching down, I grabbed Qarl's head firmly and picked it up, wincing as I did so. Behind me, the arms and legs began thrashing about once again, this time in obvious protest.

I stared down into the face I was holding. Qarl's eyes narrowed, and his face contorted with rage, his lips rapidly mouthing what I could only guess were interplanetary obscenities, but no sound could be heard. I suppose it made sense that being beheaded would tamper with one's ability to speak audibly (among other things).

Turning the head around so that I didn't have to look at his enraged face, I stepped back over to Qarl's flailing body. *There has to be a way to reattach this thing,* I thought. Cradling the head in my elbow, I reached down and grabbed hold of the body. It kicked in protest as I picked it up and examined the wrinkled neck area.

Then I felt sharp teeth press into the crook of my arm. Qarl was trying to bite me. I dropped the body and spun the head around.

"Listen, you little son of a bitch," I spat at him angrily, "I can't fix this unless you stop struggling. Knock it off!"

Qarl responded by sticking out his fat tongue at me, but his body stopped squirming. I picked it up again and resumed my concentration. I placed the head against the body—screwing it, twisting it, turning it, pushing it—in hopes that some sort of connection would take place, but the head remained just as detached as ever.

Qarl rolled his huge eyes, and his arm began tugging at my shirt. I brushed him off, trying to focus. He became more insistent, pulling harder at my shirt and mouthing something unintelligible. I pushed his arm away firmly again, peering closer at the neck region. How could I close the connection? At a loss, I let loose a defeated sigh. Qarl would not stop pulling earnestly on my shirt, and I was growing tired at this point.

Wait…grow. That was it. My shirt was made of cotton.

Moving quickly, I situated the head and neck, holding it in place with one hand while I grasped the corner of my shirt with the other and rubbed the fabric gently across the joining seam. Instantly Qarl's skin began to stretch and grow, sealing the breach without a trace. The reattachment was successful. I placed Qarl back on the floor as he stretched his neck to remove any kinks.

"Ugh, finally," he said, his annoying voice returning at last. "Don't know why it took you that long to figure it out."

I was relieved that Qarl was back to normal, but regretful at the close call I had caused. "I…I didn't know your head could come off so easily," I stammered.

Qarl looked at me sheepishly, as if slightly embarrassed by the whole situation. "Yeah, it does…if subjected to enough trauma." He felt his head all over, as if to ensure that everything was working properly.

I knew an apology was in order. "Um, I'm sorry I hit you, dude. I shouldn't have gotten so angry."

Qarl looked down at the floor and shuffled his feet. "It's ok. I'm sorry I insulted your mom."

"I didn't know 'your mom' jokes were so universal," I said with a little smile.

"Every place you can find mothers," Qarl replied, grinning, "you can find 'your mom' jokes."

With the apologies out of the way, silence reigned once again for a brief moment, until the awkwardness became too much. Qarl broke it first.

"Well…we've already lost enough time. Shall we go?" He crossed over to the panel. I nodded and followed. Qarl clapped twice, and the panel sprang open.

"Welcome to X@X!"

Chapter D

[Editor's Note: At this point in the narrative, the author chose to continue his story in poetry form. In the interest of preserving accuracy over consistency, we have presented this portion of the manuscript unaltered, with our apologies for any cognitive disturbances the shift may cause.]

Way out in space lies a land that is far,
Past the planets, the sun, and that "beetlejuice" star.
This place is so far you can't get there with cars,
Or with planes, or with trains, or by wishing on stars.
(Not even with help from those Martians on Mars!)

Beyond where the comets and ast'roids relax,
Lies an odd-shaped and rather large planet called X@X.
This X@X planet's really a neat place to be—
A place where there're many weird creatures to see!

But first let us talk 'bout this planet's odd shape:
It's not like an egg, or a ball, or a grape,
Or a marble, a pea, or a garbanzo bean.
No, X@X is like nothing that you've ever seen!
It's not round at all; no, instead it is flat,
Like it used to be something that one day went "SPLAT!"
It's shaped like a twisted, gargantuan wedge,
So that, if you weren't careful, you'd fall off the edge!

But now, let's discuss all the things that live here:
You won't find koalas, or bison, or deer,

Or monkeys, or eagles, or big kangaroos,
Or any such creature that quacks, neighs, or moos!

Near the tip of the wedge of this planet, there dwells
A creature who lives in a cave full of bells.
This creature is carefree and really quite dapper;
He's known 'round these parts as the Old Frapalapper.
Now, this Frapalapper is really quite weird,
With wings on his head and a chin on his beard.
He tastes with his eyeballs and sees with his nose
And smells with his fingers and breathes through his toes!
And he's always singing wherever he goes;
He's got a great voice, with a 12-octave range!
(I told you this creature is just a bit strange!)

And then there's the Gerfron, who lives in a home
That's made out of cardboard and old styrofoam.
His house sits on top of a snow-covered heap,
And he keeps a small flock of blue Shonkleshorn sheep.
These sheep don't grow wool; no, instead they give silk,
And orange juice instead of the usual milk!

Beyond Gerfron's home lives the Frobo-Zo-Polo.
(Unlike Frapalapper, he won't sing a solo!)
This Frobo-Zo-Polo is bouncing a yo-yo;
He'd bounce more than one if it wasn't a no-no.

[Editor's Note: At this point, the author chose—perhaps wisely— to resume the narrative in prose.]

Ok, ok, I gave it a shot, but poetry just isn't going to work for the rest of this story. (Besides, I don't even know if I rhymed "X@X" correctly. I'm still not exactly sure how that name is pronounced. Qarl gave me an evil glare every time I said it.)

Moving on…

So I'm sure you've gathered by now that X@X was like nothing I had ever seen. I won't bore you with a lengthy description, as I feel the poem was more than enough. Suffice it to say that, as Qarl and I exited the pod, many strange and weird and wonderful sights met our eyes. (Strange to me, at least; Qarl seemed rather unfazed by it all.)

We were in a city, our pod situated rather oddly in what appeared to be the central square. It was a rather busy place, with tall buildings and moving vehicles and aliens bustling about here and there. They paid us no mind, not finding it odd in the least to find two travelers stepping out of the pod and walking away. But it wasn't the aliens that grabbed my attention.

"Qarl!" I hissed, leaning forward. "There are humans here!" Indeed, there were. They were everywhere, strolling among the aliens and conversing with each other. Qarl shook his head and continued walking.

"Of course there are Humans here," he replied. "Humans aren't a species exclusive to Earth. There are Earth-Humans and there are X@X-Humans. There are a few other planets out there with Humans as well, but not as many."

I stared in awe at these kindred beings, wondering if they were exactly the same as their Earth counterparts. I was very curious to speak to one, even more so than to any of the numerous aliens roaming the city. Neither human nor alien glanced our way, however, as our little twosome didn't look much different from any other passersby on the street.

I was startled out of my distracted daze when I ran into something: it was Qarl. He had stopped abruptly in front of a small shop, and I had rear-ended him.

"Pay attention!" he snapped. "Are you hungry?"

I looked at the shop in front of us. Bright neon lights blazed out the name of the establishment: Bork's Burgers. As I read the sign, the aroma of greasy junk food wafted through the open door and into my nostrils. I cocked my head. I guess I hadn't expected something as ordinary as a burger joint in such a futuristic environment.

I nodded to Qarl and followed him into the tiny restaurant. The interior of the place looked like the inside of any burger place back home, except we typically didn't get alien customers in burger joints back on Earth.

Qarl approached the counter. Standing on tiptoes and peering over, he snapped his fingers to get a server's attention. A greenish alien stepped to the register, a burly fellow with five and a half eyes and very hairy elbows.

"What'll it be?" he drawled. Qarl tapped his fingers on the counter as he contemplated his order.

"I'll have the Borktastic Burger Deluxx with extra cheese and pikkles...oh, and hold the stardust," he instructed.

"And for your friend?"

"He'll have the daily special." Qarl turned to me. "That's fine, right?"

I shrugged and nodded. I wasn't sure what to expect in this galactic establishment. Any food was fair game, I figured.

Qarl turned back to the server. "Yes, the daily special it is."

"Ok. Now, which day would you like? Jupiter's daily special just ended a little while ago, but there are still a few mirkrons left for Saturn's special. And let's see…there's quite a bit of time left on the Mercury daily, although between you and me, we may as well call Mercury's daily special a yearly special, its day is so damn long," he chortled.

"I think I'll take the Venus daily," Qarl said after some deliberation.

"Ah, a classic! Hasn't changed since last time you were here, as a matter of fact. It's still the 10-piece BorkBites™."

"Excellent," Qarl said with a smile. "Now, name your price."

"Twenty," the server replied.

"No, forty," Qarl countered.

The server shook his head. "Twenty-five."

"Thirty-five."

"Thirty," the server insisted.

"Done!" Qarl stuck out his hand for the server to shake. He then pulled some coins out of a fold in his side and placed them on the counter. Handing us our food with a smile and 2¾ winks, the server bade us goodbye as Qarl and I went on our way. As we left the building, food in hand, I nudged my companion.

"You can haggle your price in places like that?" I asked curiously, taking a tentative nibble of a BorkBite™. *Not bad.*

"Um, yeah," Qarl replied. "How else would you pay for something? You don't expect the proprietors to be able to just set a price and demand it, do you? That's too much power in their hands and too little in ours." He paused to take a bite of his burger.

"But you haggled *up* instead of down," I enquired further. "Why?"

Qarl stopped and sighed. "Please remind me to get you a manual on our ways of life so you won't find a need to ask me a question every waking moment," he muttered. "Ok, we haggle up because the fewer coins you have, the better. Coins are heavy and dirty. Money is a burden, a necessary evil. We want as little of it as possible."

Qarl took another bite of burger. "The government taxes us by giving us coins. Shop owners set low prices so that they will receive the least amount of coins possible. We as consumers haggle up to get rid of as much as we can. That's how it works around here." He stuffed his face hungrily as we continued weaving through the crowds.

My mind was blown. I had never thought about money that way before. It was intriguing: a system where a currency's perceived value was opposite its face value. I had so many more questions about this new discovery, but Qarl quickened his pace and grabbed my hand as we turned a street corner.

"Come on, the Queen is waiting," he said briskly. "We're already late."

"I've never been to a palace before," I said excitedly. "I assume she lives in a palace, right?" As absurd as that question sounded to me, I figured at this point that I shouldn't take any fact for granted anymore, not in such a different and unpredictable environment as X@X.

Turns out I was right in asking. Qarl shook his head and muttered something that sounded like "spuhfiggus."

"Huh?"

"She lives in the SPFGS," he repeated. "The Spatial Palatial Fantastic Galactic Spectacular." He made a sweeping motion with his hand, and his eyes grew wider as he continued. "It is oh-so-grand, so beautiful, so—

well…spectacular, that a word like 'palace' demeans its splendor."

He turned to me, his face animated with intense enthusiasm. "If you've never seen a palace, my friend, then you certainly have never seen the likes of…the SPFGS!" He punctuated those last two words with appropriate dramatic flair.

As if on cue, we rounded a corner just as Qarl was completing his speech, and there before us was—well, it was the most incredibly beautiful structure I had ever seen in my life. It was an eclectic blend of architectural wonder: part castle, part palace, part mansion, part skyscraper—the comparisons were endless.

The SPFGS towered before us as Qarl and I approached, at once daunting and inviting, intimidating yet welcoming. Marble walls, towering spires, crystal columns, hanging gardens, floating fountains, shimmering lights—it was almost too much to take in. It was like something out of a fairy tale, only more beautiful and more grand. I could've sworn I heard a string quartet playing and birds twittering as I stared at the magnificent spectacle, but that part was probably my imagination.

The entire place was situated on a rise and surrounded by a colorful brick wall, each brick a distinct hue of the rainbow. In its center was a golden gate, with a winding path leading up the hill to it.

Qarl started up the path and motioned for me to follow. As we approached the gate, I couldn't help but notice the absence of any guards present. I wondered how we were going to be let in.

Once at the gate, Qarl stopped before a tiny speaker situated just off to the side. Pressing a call button, he waited for a response. With a crackle, a thin voice came over the speaker.

"State your business."

Qarl leaned forward. "This is Qarl. I'm here on official business with Her Splendiferous Majesty, Queen of the Cosmos, along with the Earth-Human she requested." He puffed out his chest as he spoke.

I smirked. Qarl clearly loved titles.

"Scan your ID," the voice said flatly. Qarl felt in the folds of his skin but couldn't seem to come up with anything.

"Blast!" he exclaimed to me. "I must've left it behind on the Ken.10 when we had to evacuate." He turned back to the speaker. "Um, I don't have my ID on my person. But we are in a rush. The Queen is expecting us. Just let us in."

The speaker crackled again. "I'm sorry. If you do not have your ID, then you must speak a twister."

Qarl sighed impatiently. "Look, I don't have time for this. It's me. Qarl. Just let me and my companion in."

"I'm sorry, it's protocol. You and your friend both must speak a twister."

Qarl was growing impatient. He leaned in closer to the speaker until his lips were practically touching it.

"Listen, you little low-level employee," he growled. "You are delaying the Queen's official business. I could have you fired. Is that what you want? Huh?" He banged on the speaker. "I know it's you, Brenda. Quit being such a pain in the torgon and open up!"

The speaker crackled once more. "Speak the twister or go away." Brenda sure was insistent. Qarl rolled his eyes and released a frustrated sigh.

"Fine," he muttered. Squinting his eyes with concentration, he faced the speaker squarely and spoke:

"The shaman's shapeless shadow shocked the sheepish shepherd's sheep." This he said with some difficulty, although he managed it fairly well. "Happy now?" he shouted into the speaker.

"That will be sufficient," Brenda replied. "And now, your friend."

Qarl turned to me. "Ok, it's your turn," he said. "Say a twister. Any twister. It just has to be clear and intelligible when you say it."

I was a bit nervous at this. I had never been good at tongue twisters, and I was afraid of what might happen should I fail. As a result of this stress, my mind temporarily blanked.

"Uh, I don't remember any. What should I do? Why do I need to say a tongue twister anyway?" I broke into a panicked sweat and began to crack my knuckles nervously. Qarl reached up, grabbed my shoulders with his long arms, and pulled me down to his level.

"Calm down," he said, shaking me. "It's just a security measure. Well, more of a convenience measure actually. The Queen has limited time with a lot on her schedule. She only wishes to speak with those who are swift of tongue."

"I thought you had an appointment. You are expected, aren't you?" I asked.

"Yes, I am, and normally my ID would get me right in, but this hag"—he paused briefly and looked disdainfully at the speaker—"this hag won't let me in without it, so she is treating me as if I were any other visitor." He released his grip on my shoulders. "Now, just breathe, think of the simplest twister you can, and go for it."

I had fully relaxed by now, and my mind was clear. Stepping forward to the speaker, I cleared my throat and spoke:

"Boy toad."

There was a pause. Then the speaker crackled. "Invalid response. That is not a twister."

Now I was the one growing impatient and more than a little annoyed. "Oh yeah?" I countered defiantly into the speaker. "Try saying it ten times fast."

There was another, longer pause. Then the speaker crackled tentatively, the voice quiet this time.

"Welcome to the SPFGS."

With a squeak, a creak, and a metallic shriek, the golden gates sprang open. Qarl grabbed my arm, and we rushed inside.

Once we were past the colorful walls, my eyes were met with the most beautiful gardens imaginable. Fruit trees, bright flowers, and the greenest grass I had ever seen stretched out of sight in either direction, encircling the central structure. Little robotic gardeners tended the grounds: trimming trees, pruning bushes, and mowing the lawns. One waved at me as I passed. I wanted to stop and analyze these little machines, but Qarl pulled me along at a brisk pace.

After passing quickly through the large courtyard, we stood before the entrance to the SPFGS itself. A tall wooden door was all that stood between us and the interior of this splendid place. This door, while clean and brightly polished, still looked oddly primitive compared to the grandeur and futuristic marvel of the rest of the compound.

There was no bell, no button, no speaker...Qarl just reached up and knocked. Apparently, Brenda had sent word ahead that we were there, because the door flew open immediately and we were ushered in by an alien guard.

If I thought the exterior of this place was grand, I was not prepared for what the interior held. The design was a perfect blend of traditional opulence and futuristic convenience.

We were standing in a large hall.

[Editor's Note: Here the manuscript was smudged to the point of illegibility, so the description of the extravagant hall will have to live in the reader's imagination.]

We were ready to enter the Queen's chamber. The double doors swung open, and Qarl and I stepped through. My mouth opened in awe. The Queen's quarters were even more lavish than the great hall.

Everything was purple, from the silk drapes hanging in the windows to the plush carpet that stretched wall to wall. A chandelier hung from the ceiling, the bulbs covered in tinted violet glass. Between two windows in the center of the far wall, a small throne stood, unassuming in its simplicity compared with the luxuriance of the rest of the space.

The entire chamber was immaculately kept. Ladies-in-waiting flitted about, tending to various duties, each one dressed in a purple apron. One carried a tray of delicately painted china while another wielded a feather duster made of purple plumage.

At one corner of the room, a tall figure stood, her back to us, staring out one of the windows. Thick brown tresses cascaded down her shoulders and over a sparkling purple cape that reached to the floor. She stood motionless, as if aware of the activity in the room but indifferent to it. No crown adorned her head, but I knew that this majestic-looking woman had to be the Queen.

I elbowed Qarl and raised an eyebrow. He nodded to me before turning and calling to the woman across the room.

"Your Magniferous Queenship, Qarl reporting as requested."

He bowed low as he spoke, and I followed suit, although I kept my head up and my gaze fixed curiously on the Queen. I couldn't wait to see how beautiful she looked.

There was a pause…then the cape rustled and stirred as the Queen slowly turned, her royal figure pivoting gracefully as she moved to face us. My jaw dropped, and I staggered backward a step.

The Queen of the Cosmos was completely nude!

Chapter DD

...qwertyuiopasdfghjklzxcvbnmmnbvcxzlkjhgfdsapoiuytrewq...

Sorry, but that's about what was running through my mind as I gazed in shock at the Queen. I certainly hadn't expected the utter lack of clothing.

She was a beautiful woman, to be sure, with gentle eyes, flawless skin, and just about the most perfect breasts I had ever seen. She was humanlike in most aspects of her appearance, but from the place where her nipples would have been emanated two bright points of light, like stars shining from her breasts. The Queen cast a truly regal figure as she stood poised before us, her glittering cape draping off her bare shoulders and around her wide hips.

I quickly lowered my gaze as the Queen stepped forward. She proffered her hand to Qarl, and he gently kissed it. Then she spoke.

"It is good to see you back, Qarl," she purred. Her voice was gentle and soothing, like silk wrapped in velvet. "And who did you bring with you?" She nodded my direction.

"This, Your Gracious Grace, is the Earth-namuH—I mean, Earth-Human—you requested. Sorry, it's the dysleqsia again."

The Queen smiled kindly. "There is no need to apologize, Qarl." She turned to me. "I am most pleased to meet you."

I nodded stupidly and blushed, lowering my head to avoid eye contact. I was rather uncomfortable, not sure how to act in the presence of a beautiful naked queen.

Stepping in front of me, she lifted my chin gently to meet her gaze. Her violet eyes were mesmerizing, seductive, and terrifyingly charming. A smile played at the corners of her glossy lips.

"Don't be ill at ease," she breathed softly. "You are most welcome here. Relax, and I will explain everything momentarily."

With a wave of her hand, the Queen turned and walked to her throne, her cape sweeping grandly behind her. Two servants rushed to place chairs behind Qarl and me. Taking a seat, the Queen nodded for us to do the same. It turned out that her throne was on wheels and motorized, for with a press of a button on her armrest, the Queen glided her throne closer to us, leaving small tracks in the fluffy carpet. Folding her hands on her lap, she leaned forward and spoke.

"Now," she began, looking at me, "I know you are wondering why I requested that Qarl bring you to meet me." I nodded. "Well, it's a bit of a story, but I shall do my best to enlighten you as quickly as possible."

π π π π π

The Queen launched into a lengthy backstory to give me a broader picture of the situation at hand. Apparently, despite her title as Queen of the Cosmos, there existed another force more powerful than she in space. Tucked far away at the very edge of the known universe was a planet called Hob. This planet was home to two large aliens named Asdf and Jkl, who truly controlled the entire universe and everything in it. In practice, however, they were a fairly lazy pair of aliens and preferred to let the rest of the cosmos get by on their own, without much interference.

Asdf and Jkl amused themselves most of the time by employing advanced technology to play games with the planets: rolling them through space like marbles, juggling them, using them to play popular competitive sports like billiards and bowling, and otherwise utilizing the universe as their giant playground. Asteroids, meteors, and comets were also playthings of theirs, Qarl and I being unlucky enough to have come in the path of one of the latter on our expedition over.

Despite the seemingly reckless nature of Asdf and Jkl's treatment of the universe, however, very little harm was ever caused by their games, and aliens and humans alike accepted the bizarre situation as normal. And indeed, it was, for this arrangement had been in place for unknown eons. In fact, any departure from this peculiar way the universe was run would have been cause for alarm.

But something did change.

As mentioned earlier, X@X was a rather odd-shaped planet. Unlike most planets—which tend to have a spherical configuration—X@X was shaped like a giant wedge of cheese. Due to its strange form, the planet was never included in the Games of Hob, as it was difficult for Asdf and Jkl to find a suitable use for it. The residents of X@X didn't mind this lack of participation, however, for a deep distrust toward the great Asdf and Jkl simmered in the depths of X@X. Some of the other planets shared the sentiment as well, but the feeling was perhaps centered deepest on X@X, as it was where the universe's second-in-command resided, the Queen of the Cosmos.

You see, as the de facto ruler of the cosmos, the Queen felt a deep responsibility to be wary of any and all threats to order and survival. She had never been placed in charge by the rulers of Hob; rather, she had risen to power to fill a need that their apathy couldn't satisfy. It was she who kept order and meted out justice for the denizens of space.

Taking practical rule of the universe out of necessity, the Queen did not assume that Asdf and Jkl wouldn't ever harm it in any way, despite their technical positions as head rulers of the cosmos. From her standpoint, their isolated nature and general indifference toward running the universe could be both assuring and concerning. And so, from a distance, she watched them as intently as she watched any potential threat, with a guarded mistrust. There was never any uprising, never any revolution, never any coup, and never any attack from either side, but the Queen was always on the lookout for any trouble from Hob, and now she believed she had found some.

Word from a reputable source had reached the Queen's ears that Asdf and Jkl were growing annoyed with the "useless" members of their universe cluttering the cosmos. Broken asteroids, burned-out comets, misshapen planets—these had no use in their games and were only taking up space. There was talk that Hob was going to undertake a purge—a cleansing of sorts—to dispose of what they could not use in their sporting amusements.

X@X was one of those "useless" things.

Since most of the alien population of the universe had a certain level of fear toward Asdf and Jkl, the Queen did not wish to raise any alarm and cause mass hysteria, but she knew she had to do something about the imminent threat. That's when she was struck with an idea, an idea involving a certain planet called Earth.

Now, everyone knew that Earth was Asdf and Jkl's favorite planet. They played with it often and treated it gently. No one was exactly sure why they preferred Earth so much, but it may have had something to do with how very different it was from all the other planets. At any rate, the Queen thought that if she could send a resident of Earth to Hob, this person could talk with the two great aliens and convince them to spare X@X, as they would be sure to listen to anyone visiting from their favorite plaything.

It was a risky maneuver, as it had been a great while since any creature, alien or human, had dared to approach Hob and disturb its residents. But the Queen, wishing to avoid a universal conflict, knew that this was X@X's only recourse and hope for survival.

π π π π π

The Queen leaned back in her throne after the exhaustive explanation. I sat frozen in my chair, unsure of what to think. My mind was a blur as I tried to process all this information. It was as if my entire world had been turned upside down as I realized that the universe was nothing like I had been told growing up. I felt small, insignificant, and I wasn't even sure of what reality consisted of anymore.

I just had one question.

"Why me?" I managed to choke out in a whisper. "Out of all the people on Earth, why was I chosen?"

The Queen rose from her royal throne and stepped over to me. Her shining breasts illuminated my face with a gentle glow as she stood before me. Placing her hand on my shoulder, she spoke softly.

"You were chosen by prophecy." She clapped her hands suddenly, startling me out of my stupor. "Bring in the Keeper and the Prophet!" she called out.

A bell was rung, and a door at the far end of the chamber was opened. Through it stepped a young man about my age and build. To my surprise, he was wearing jeans, a T-shirt, and a blue baseball cap—rather casual clothing compared to the opulence of his surroundings. As he approached our little group, I noticed that he carried a tiny golden cage attached to a blue ribbon that hung from his wrist. The Queen gestured toward him as she introduced us.

"This is Bobby," she said. "He is the Keeper of the Prophet. And this"—she pointed at the miniature cage—"is the Prophet." She motioned for me to step closer, and I leaned in. "Meet Wonder Wasp."

I jerked back. *A wasp!?!* I didn't like wasps. I had had one too many bad experiences with them as a kid. Sensing my apprehension, Bobby spoke up.

"Oh, it's ok," he said reassuringly, his voice calm and soothing. "Wonder Wasp is quite intelligent and tame. He is here to prophesy, not to terrorize."

Cautiously, I leaned forward again until my nose was practically touching the cage. Peering inside, I took a closer look at the Prophet.

A large wasp crouched on the floor of the cage, a gentle buzzing vibrating his striped body. His large compound eyes studied me carefully, and his antennae twitched with a sort of fiendish intelligence. I was both curious and intimidated.

"How does Wonder Wasp—you know—prophesy?" I ventured.

Bobby smiled warmly. "The Prophet speaks through his venom," he explained. "But only those with the blood to receive it can interpret the message contained therein. I happen to come from a special breed of humans. We are called Keepers, and we alone can decipher the meaning of what Wonder Wasp delivers through his stinger."

"Sooooo…he has to sting you?"

"Of course," Bobby replied with a grin. "But it barely hurts. Here, let me show you."

He reached down and opened a small golden door on the cage. I stepped back a respectful distance. I didn't particularly feel like getting jabbed with a prophecy that day.

Bobby placed his finger by the cage opening, and the wasp slowly stepped out onto his hand. Raising his hand to his face, Bobby closed his eyes and whispered something unintelligible. His thumb gently stroked the wasp, back and forth, back and forth. Wonder Wasp flicked his wings and cocked an antenna in response.

There was a pause.

Then, with a quiver of his abdomen, Wonder Wasp drove his rear end downward and into Bobby's finger. I winced in sympathy, but Bobby never flinched. After a few seconds, the Prophet withdrew his stinger, and Bobby lowered him back into his cage with one smooth motion.

"It is as he prophesied before," Bobby said. "This Earth-human is indeed the one."

The Queen nodded in approval and motioned for Bobby to step aside. I, however, was admittedly a bit skeptical. How could a wasp prophesy? I mean, granted, I had seen my share of weirdness on this planet, but a prophesying wasp? *Come on.*

For all I knew, this wasp could be a relative of the wasp family I had kicked out of my mom's favorite tree last summer. They had built a big ol' nest, and I had taken a can of hairspray and a blowtorch to it. Ah, it was beautiful. It was possible that this "Wonder Wasp" was a distant relative, out to exact his revenge upon the human that had so brutally destroyed his loved ones. Why else would I be picked for this mission? Out of all the humans on my planet, why was I chosen?

I saw no logical reason for my selection…but I also saw no logical basis for a vengeful wasp with a calculated plan either, so I just decided to keep going along with whatever was going on in this weird part of the universe.

"Very well," I said with a shrug. "I accept your mission. I will go to Hob and speak with Asdf and Jkl."

A delighted smile spread over the Queen's face. "We are in your debt, young man," she said.

"I don't know how persuasive I'll be," I cautioned, not wanting to get their hopes up. "But I'll do my best."

"Have faith in your abilities, my friend," the Queen said sweetly. "Perhaps this journey will end with success if we will it so."

Our little meeting over, the Queen instructed me to go with Bobby as she adjourned to another chamber with Qarl for a debriefing on the details of our trip over. I waved goodbye to my little blue pal and followed Bobby out of the royal chamber and down another hallway, making it a point to walk on the side opposite Bobby's barb-butted companion.

As we walked, Bobby pointed out various areas of interest in the SPFGS, playing quite the enthusiastic tour guide. He was a friendly guy and, despite being some mystic channel for prophecy, actually seemed quite down-to-earth. He and I hit it off tremendously as we strolled through the halls, chatting about our respective lives in two very different areas of the universe.

Bobby paused in front of a partially open door. Inside, I could hear the drone of a female voice reciting numbers and figures while dozens of pencils scratched dutifully in response.

"This is the classroom where all the children of the SPFGS study," Bobby explained in a low voice, careful not to disturb the occupants within. "Madame Stringent provides the best tutelage, although she can be quite the bitch, if you know what I mean." He grinned widely. "I have felt myself on the wrong end of her wrath many a time growing up here."

I peeked through the door crack but couldn't catch a glimpse of the stern woman. All I could hear was the chilling monotone of her voice as she listed figure after figure for the weary students to solve:

"1+19+13+0+6+17+15+4+13+0+19+11+17+15+24+2+14…"

I turned to Bobby. "Is she human?" I asked curiously.

"Barely," Bobby joked. He pulled me away from the door, and we continued our excursion through the halls.

"So, tell me," he said after a few moments of silence, "what do you think of our queen?"

I flushed a little. "She's very nice," I replied cautiously, "and extremely beautiful." I stole a glance sideways at Bobby. He caught my eye and grinned.

"You want to know why she's naked, don't you?" he said, a knowing gleam in his eye. I lowered my gaze and nodded sheepishly.

"It's ok," he continued. "Many visitors from your neck of the universe wonder the same thing. It's quite simple, really. As you have by now noticed, there are humans here on X@X—as well as on some other planets—just like on your

Earth, but there are a few key differences between our species.

"For one, some of us humans here have different powers or skills than your people do. Secondly, unlike on Earth, the female gender isn't as sexualized as the male gender. Therefore, a female human can go practically nude if she wishes, while it is against the law for male humans to even go topless. So don't go taking your shirt off in public if you know what's good for you." He chuckled as he said this last sentence.

I gulped. This was a new development. I was at once struck with a profound giddiness at the potential amount of female flesh I could be exposed to, but also gripped with a tense nervousness at the unaccustomed modesty regulations imposed so suddenly upon me. I had never had to think before about how I dressed or how much skin I showed in public. What was considered acceptable? What if I unwittingly broke the law? What was the penalty? As if sensing my thoughts, Bobby spoke up.

"Hey, just watch what I wear, and you can't go wrong." He smiled reassuringly, and I relaxed slightly.

Changing the subject, I began asking Bobby more about Hob, Asdf and Jkl, the games, and how it all related to X@X while he continued pointing out rooms and items of interest as we walked.

"It's a shame that things are changing for you guys here," I said sympathetically. "How soon do you think events will come to a head?"

"Very soon, I'm afraid," Bobby replied, a grimness in his voice.

"There's gotta be a way to buy some time," I said earnestly. Bobby stopped.

"Oh, you want to buy some time? Here, the gift shop is right up ahead." He took me by the arm and pulled me around a corner and into a small shop off one of the halls. It was set up much like an airport or hospital gift shop, with many little trinkets and souvenirs for the various visitors that came through the SPFGS.

I was confused. "Wait, what are you doing?" I sputtered.

Bobby stopped in front of a glass display case filled with vials. "You said you wanted to buy some time. Well, here you go," he replied, gesturing at the case.

"That's just an expression," I said, still confused. "You mean you can actually purchase time here?"

"Certainly. That's what's in those little vials. Of course, the Queen doesn't like for Time to be tampered with too much, so she limits the amount that can be bought and sold. Usually only a few mirkrons come in a vial, but they sure are fun to play with. I've even gotten out of a pinch or two with one of these."

Bobby picked up a vial and handed it to me. It was made out of tempered glass and contained a swirling, purplish smoke.

"That one contains mirkrons," Bobby pointed out. "And these ones"—he reached and grabbed a vial full of swirling green smoke—"are mircrims. A mircrim is a reversible time unit." He passed the vial to me, and I compared it with the one in my hand.

"Why would you want time to go backward?" I asked.

Bobby shrugged. "I don't know. Sometimes life is just more interesting in reverse."

"So how do these things work?" I asked, examining the vials. "How do you...you know...turn them on?"

Bobby laughed and took the purple vial from me. "It's easy," he replied. "You just remove the cap and wave the dial in a spectral pattern." He glanced around quickly. "Here, I'll haggle for this later. Let me just show you."

Positioning himself so that he was facing me, he held the vial out in front of him and popped the cap off with his thumb. The purple smoke began to rush toward the opening, eager to escape.

Bobby grasped the vial firmly and began swirling it rapidly in an odd pattern above and around and between the two of us. A seemingly endless stream of purple smoke billowed from the vial with a hiss as he did so, until my entire view was shrouded in a dense cloud of color. Only Bobby was visible through the purple fog that surrounded us.

"Now, wait a moment," Bobby said, lowering the vial. "The smoke will clear soon."

He was right. The purple cloud gradually dissipated as the smoke dissolved into the air. I could now see my surroundings clearly again...only, everything was different. My entire view was tinted with a purplish hue, as if I were looking through a colored lens. The bustling sounds of the shop that had previously invaded my ears were now lowered to a dull, low-pitched hum.

But what was even more alarming was the fact that every moving thing in that shop was now frozen in place. Customers were paused midstride in the aisles, mouths open in midconversation. Shop employees stood paralyzed at the front counter with money and receipts in hand, the papers rigid with not a flutter to be seen. My entire surroundings had been frozen in place and doused in purple. Only Bobby moved and looked normal.

"What's going on?" I questioned Bobby. "Are you seeing what I'm seeing?"

"Sure am," he said with a grin. "The effect will wear off shortly, but let me explain to you what is happening. It appears that we have given ourselves extra units of time. See how you and I continue to move while Space and Time around us seem frozen in place?"

I nodded, and he continued. "Now, everyone knows that you can't actually add or subtract time without creating a ripple effect that changes the linearity of the overall Timeline of the Universe and affects everything within it. So, for the vial of mirkrons to affect only us, it merely alters our *perception* of the existing span of Time by physically speeding up everything within this cloud of smoke.

"From our point of view, the surrounding world has slowed almost to a stop, but in reality, you and I are just moving very rapidly physically within the parameters of the smoke. Time has not *actually* sped up or slowed down for us or them, nor has it been added; rather, our physical capabilities and movement within this cloud have increased in speed.

"What this does is allow us to experience Time on a much smaller scale. We are essentially able to 'zoom in' on the linear model of Time and experience smaller increments as if they were longer increments. We are able to accomplish more physically in the same period of Time than we were before. Follow me so far?"

"I think so," I replied. "Go on."

"Now, I'm sure you notice that you don't *feel* as if you are moving any faster than normal, and here's why. This preservation of the mind's paradigm that our bodies are still traveling normally through Time is accomplished by our brain wave activity being increased in conjunction with the physical properties of everything within the smoke being sped up. Therefore, we still feel that we are experiencing Time at a normal pace, while our eyes tell us that our surroundings have slowed. To us, it is they who have slowed down, rather than we who have sped up.

"This brainwave alteration is enhancing the perception that we have additional time on our hands by making us feel that Space and Time around us have paused momentarily while we are still able to function normally. The process is very similar to how you can fall asleep for an hour and yet have a dream that seems to last a day. Your brain is able to process information much faster, and so your perception of the passage of Time is altered.

"So, in essence, the addition of time is merely an illusion: we 'see' that Time is passing by at a fraction of the normal rate while our consciousness retains its perspective of normalcy. In reality, both we and the world around us are living through the same few mirkrons simultaneously, but we in the smoke *perceive* it to be much longer through this process of being physically sped up while being kept unaware of the change. Thus, we've essentially added time to our awareness while Time remains unchanged in reality. Make sense?"

My mind was whirling with this influx of information, but I attempted to summarize what he had just said in order to make sense of it.

"So the speeding up is what fake-adds the time, and the alteration of the brain waves is what makes us feel that the time was added?" I asked tentatively.

"Exactly," Bobby replied with a nod. "What we are really doing is 'squeezing in' extra time by being able to move incredibly fast, albeit while not being aware of it. But Time remains unaltered overall."

I nodded. I was starting to grasp the concept but didn't want to think too much deeper about it for fear that I'd unravel more puzzling questions. By this time, the smoke's effect had worn off, and my surroundings appeared normal once again. As the last vestiges of purple drifted silently into the surrounding shadows and corners, Bobby, Wonder Wasp, and I exited the shop.

π π π π π

After showing me a few more places of interest around the SPFGS, Bobby escorted me to my sleeping quarters, where I was to stay until the Queen had finished preparations for my great voyage to Hob. To my surprise, the room was virtually identical to my bedroom back home. The bed, the closet, the desk, the window—everything was almost exactly the same. I turned to Bobby in speechless amazement. He grinned at me.

"Qarl gave us the details for the layout of your bedroom. He thought you'd be more comfortable in a place that reminded you of home."

That son of a gun, I chuckled to myself. Qarl could be a royal pain in the ass, but he definitely had a heart. I walked through the room, inspecting every accurate detail. A couple things seemed off though. I cocked my head at a poster on the wall.

"Who are the syoB teertskcaB?" I wondered.

"Oh, Qarl may have gotten a few items backward. He's dysleqsic," Bobby explained. "Dysleqsia is similar to the Earth disorder dyslexia but with a few differences: it's a rare genetic disorder unique to specific regions and results in the sufferer reading, writing, and even speaking in reverse or out of order. Qarl is able to manage it quite well, but it occasionally slips through."

"I see," I replied. This explained some of Qarl's previous actions I had witnessed.

"Well," Bobby continued, "get some sleep. Someone will be by to get you in the morning. You'll be briefed on plan details as soon as they are finalized." I thanked him, and he left, closing the door behind him.

I was being left alone for the longest time since leaving my safe bedroom back on Earth...and in a similar-looking place. My experience had gone full circle: alone in my room back home to alone in this place that looked so much like it.

I stretched out on the bed and surveyed the space around me. Indeed, everything seemed so familiar, and yet an ache of loneliness pressed against my heart. I was surprised to discover that I was really starting to miss home, despite my prior misgivings about returning to the house on Sickamore Street. Ironically, the sense of familiarity about my current surroundings only served to exacerbate the feelings of loneliness. I actually felt more isolated now than I had when I was stranded on the doomed Ken.10. Funny how the mind works.

I didn't have too much time to feel homesick, however: my mind was too full with all the weird events that had occurred over the past...day? I chuckled to myself. After being hurtled through space, thrust through time, and transported to a foreign planet, I wasn't even sure of the passage of time anymore. Exactly how long ago had it been since Qarl suctioned himself to my window? Had it been a day? A few days? A few hours? I couldn't be sure, but I almost didn't care. I had already given up trying to fully understand the quirky happenings I found myself surrounded with.

I was too wired to sleep at the moment, so I turned to the nightstand, hoping to find some reading material inside one of the drawers. I had left some comic books in my nightstand back home. I wondered if Qarl had noticed that detail.

Alas, he had not. A lone magazine stared up at me from inside the dusty drawer. Disappointed, I picked it up and leafed through it unenthusiastically while flopping back on the bed. It was a home improvement magazine, which I had always found to be in the top three of Most Boring Magazine Types. There were few things in this world I wanted less than to learn how to build a solid-oak china cabinet with arabesque carvings and chamfered edges. Oh, recessed lighting and chrome faucets can spruce up your kitchen with a modern feel? You don't say.

At least this borefest is putting me to sleep, I thought, yawning, as I flipped past yet another ad for a super-duper adhesive that could stop all your leaks, seal all your joints, bond all your surfaces, save all your bad relationships…

Something tickled my arm. I jerked and brushed at it. Out of the corner of my eye, I saw a shadow fly past me with a low-pitched hum. I whirled and looked at the window; the curtains were swaying gently. *Great,* I thought. Someone had left the window open, and a bug had found its way in.

I hated bugs. They simultaneously annoyed and scared me. I stood up to shut the window and was just returning to bed when a loud buzzing rushed past my ear. Jumping back, I swiped furiously at the side of my head.

I could hear a *plunk* as the insect body-slammed itself into the window. A dismayed buzz followed, which I interpreted as insect-speak for "what the fuck!?!" at finding the window closed. *Sorry, sucker,* I thought. *Shouldn't have flown in here and bothered me. You're going down!*

Arming myself with the home improvement magazine and a determined face, I crept toward the window. It would be no great loss to ruin this piece of literature with insect guts, I figured, as I continued to approach the window slowly, rolling the magazine tightly in my hands. A curtain obscured my view of the intruder, but I could hear the confused buzzing as the insect continued to headbutt the window desperately. I was almost upon him.

I reached up slowly and grasped the curtain with one hand, the other arm raising the *Interplanetary Home Improvement Guide*—my weapon of war—above my head. This beast was buzzing his last buzz.

With one swift motion, I swept the curtain aside and brought my sword of wrath down hard upon the annoying pest. But right before the thick paper connected with the fragile body, I caught a flash of black and yellow...and I knew. The realization swept over me in a hot wave, and I broke out into a spontaneous sweat.

It was Wonder Wasp.

I couldn't believe it. I began to ask myself how he had ended up on my window even while my brain was processing the answer. My mind saw it all now in crystal clear slow motion: Bobby and I entering the chamber...Bobby setting the golden cage down on the desk in the corner while he pointed out details of the room...Bobby leaving and closing the door, no cage hanging from his wrist! It all made sense now, but it was a fraction of a second too late. There was no way to stop the downward momentum of my arm.

I was about to kill Wonder Wasp.

As if detached from my own body, I saw the arm continue its deadly course toward the highly respected, highly valuable insect prophet. I cringed, anticipating the blow I was powerless to stop. As I watched in horror, the magazine struck Wonder Wasp squarely across the back, flinging his boldly striped body unceremoniously against the window. An audible gasp swept from my throat as I staggered backward, my world still moving in shocked slow motion.

Shaken, I stared down at the magazine clutched firmly in my hand. The gorgeous model selling toilets on the back cover was no longer gorgeous. Her flawless skin was now marred with wasp guts. For a moment, I marveled that she still kept a valiant smile plastered on her face, despite the circumstances. I shook myself from this reverie, however, and my thoughts turned with a rush to Wonder Wasp. I looked around frantically for him.

Then I saw him. He crouched precariously on the lower windowsill, his wings drooping. A faint frustrated buzzing emitted from his trembling body. I watched in part terror and part wonder as his rear end gyrated in circles. I think he was trying to tell me I had done something wrong. Or he was trying to put a curse on me. Regardless, I felt bad, and as I stood watching, he ceased to move.

Forgetting for a moment my former fears, I gently picked him up and cradled him in my palm. I thought I saw him breathe his last, and I felt a twinge of regret. I stroked him gently, as I had seen Bobby do. I even allowed my thumb to stray over his tail end, knowing the poor creature was dead and could no longer prophesy.

How wrong I was!

Apparently, Wonder Wasp had a bit of life left in him. Apparently, he also wanted to take part in one final prophecy, for, with a flutter of his wings, he stirred suddenly and discharged the fiery contents of his quivering butt into my thumb.

All twinges of regret gone, I shook the miscreant off my throbbing hand and crushed him soundly with my boot. But as soon as my boot hit his fragile body with a sickening *squish,* the full purport of what I had done smacked me in the face. I stared at the gory remnants of Wonder Wasp grimly and told myself that it was for the best, that I had mercifully put him out of his misery.

But inside I knew that Bobby would never forgive me.

Chapter E

My heart was pumping fast as I contemplated what to do about the murder I had just committed. I knew that Wonder Wasp's death would be discovered eventually, but I could not risk being found out as the culprit. I was stranded on a foreign planet that operated under different laws than I was used to. For all I knew, torture and death could await the person who dared to end the life of a winged prophet. It was essential that no one discover that I was that person.

Bending down slowly, I gently scraped up Wonder Wasp's mutilated body with the magazine. I stepped to the window, opened it carefully, and discarded the Prophet's remains quickly into the dark void outside. Upon spotting the golden cage on the desk where Bobby had left it, I grabbed it and chucked it outside as well, hoping to remove all traces of Wonder Wasp's presence from my room.

After shutting the window firmly, I drew the curtains closed, replaced the magazine inside the nightstand drawer, and stretched out upon my bed once more. My mind was racing so terribly that it took a few minutes for my nerves to calm down, but gradually my exhausted body won over, and I slipped into a deep sleep.

π π π π π

The next few days passed by fairly uneventfully. The Queen and Qarl were preparing for the great voyage to Hob, and Bobby was busy with matters of his own, which left me free to roam about the SPFGS. Thankfully, Wonder Wasp's death hadn't been discovered, and, after a day or two of mental agony, I soon forgot all about the stinging prophet.

Unfortunately, as grand as the SPFGS was, exploring it was rather like touring an art museum. In other words, quite boring. There weren't any secret passageways or rooms that I could find, and most humans or aliens I encountered were too busy to stop and talk.

I soon grew tired of wandering the large halls by myself, so I took to sitting in on a few of Madame Stringent's classes. All the children of the SPFGS—alien or human, from elementary to college age, whether their parents were nobility or employee—attended the classes of Madame Stringent. While a bit apprehensive at subjecting myself willingly to her chilling demeanor, I was confident that I could handle the bitch if I needed to.

Madame Stringent was a tall bony woman with a beaky nose and a jutting chin that probably could've been used as a weapon if needed. Her favorite colors vacillated between gray, brown, and black, and she always dressed in a draping gown of one of those hues. Now, mind you, these gowns didn't drape in any sort of attractive way. No, they draped in more of a gunnysack, "can't quite tell the shape of the thing they're covering" kind of way. The only skin that these garments permitted showing was her hands and her face. Not even her neck and wrists escaped the dark folds of cloth.

Madame Stringent's teaching style was stern and rather eccentric. She regularly alternated between barking screeches and a chilling monotone, often surprising the students with her rapid switches between the two approaches. Not content to remain at the front of the classroom either, she was constantly on the move, gliding amongst desks and peering at each student's work as she made her way in sweeping patterns across the room and back. Who needs eyes in the back of your head when you're constantly on the move?

The first class I chose to sit in happened to be a science class. It was rather fortuitous that I had chosen this particular day to audit, because Madame Stringent happened to be discussing the nature of sound in space, an issue that Qarl had corrected me on earlier when we were arguing in the pod. I had always been taught that sound couldn't travel in space, but Madame Stringent was about to set me straight.

"Class, yesterday we learned about noble gases and their dishonorable counterparts," she droned, tapping her long fingers on her desk and scanning the classroom with her roving eyes. "Today we will discuss the ways that sound travels in space. A common misconception that Earth-humans have is that it is impossible for sound to travel in space."

Here she looked directly at me, as if the blame for this error that my planet operated under rested on my shoulders. I shrugged and stared back, waiting for her to continue. After a brief pause, she did.

"However, this is not true. Sound can indeed travel through space, but it must have a passport in order to do so—a passport issued by the Queen. Hold all questions!" she barked suddenly, spotting a student in the back row raising his hand. "I will take questions when I am through with the explanation."

The hand lowered quickly, and Madame Stringent's gaze returned to sweeping the room. Dropping back to her low drone, she resumed the lesson.

"Sound indeed can travel through space with a passport. However, sound is very weak compared to the other forces of the universe. It does not take much to destroy or distort it. Therefore, the Queen is reluctant to issue such passports indiscriminately. Most often, the passport is given with the stipulation that the sound may travel only when carried and supported by a stream of air. This ensures that the sound arrives safely and unharmed to its destination.

"This also has led to the misconception by many"—she glared at me again—"that sound cannot travel in the absence of a medium such as air. Sound does indeed have the ability to travel whenever and wherever it will without assistance, but it is often banned from doing so for its own safety."

Another tentative hand went up. This time, Madame Stringent acknowledged it positively.

"What about the planet Daanjurz?" a female student queried. "It is rumored that it is a land of no sound whatsoever."

"This is true," Madame Stringent agreed flatly. "It is an incredibly formidable place and potentially fatal to any sound that would travel in the vicinity. The Queen has banned any and all sound in the area of Daanjurz. Its residents communicate by means of visual streams of words that come out of the speaker's mouth and float over to the recipient, where they can be read."

A few of the students uttered some *ooh*s and *aah*s at the thought of using this unique form of communication. Madame Stringent shushed them quickly.

"Such a method, as novel as it may seem, does have its drawbacks," she explained. "For instance, the speaker must be sure to direct her stream of words accurately toward her target, else it will go off course and be intercepted or lost.

Conversational privacy is virtually nonexistent as well, as anyone can read a stream in midair. In addition, one must be careful not to cross her stream with another's, as words may become jumbled and the message obscured or changed. Speaking in large crowds is very difficult, as you can imagine." The students nodded.

"And now!" she screeched suddenly, causing the entire class to collectively jump in their seats. "If someone would go get the vacuum cleaner from the janitor's closet, I will demonstrate how sound can travel in a vacuum." With a snap of her fingers, she sent one of the students off to fetch the cleaner, and the lesson resumed.

Such was the nature of the classes I attended. Oddly, Madame Stringent taught every single one of them, ranging from basic science and mathematics to planet politics and X@Xisms. The textbooks required for these classes ranged from *A History of Hob* to *The SPFGS Speller*, none of which I cared to obtain from the gift shop, despite Madame Stringent's repeated insistence that I do so. I knew I was going to be gone shortly, and I had no interest in investing myself more into schoolwork or study than I had to. This was supposed to be my summer break from college, after all.

Teaching a myriad of classes was not the only activity Madame Stringent indulged in around the SPFGS. You see, she was a fiercely conservative woman, and her obsession with prudence and piety bordered on religious. She often took it upon herself to patrol the grounds, putting an immediate stop to any activity that she deemed inappropriate. Male and female, human and alien, staff and student alike felt her stern reprimand as she criticized and controlled every aspect of their lives that she could, from dress to music to entertainment.

When an offense was discovered, Madame Stringent often resorted to various tactics intended to shame the offender. She would dramatically describe how "grieved" she was over the horrifying nature of the impropriety in question. And indeed, there seemed to be much to grieve about around the SPFGS.

In one of the dark towers on the grounds, Madame Stringent would frequently hold grieving parties with her best friends, Greta and Gretchen. Often, scores of other women would be invited. The women would pore over raunchy magazines, scandalous tabloids, and racy photos—and grieve. They would hold grieving contests, each woman trying to out-grieve the others. They would argue over whose child was the most rebellious or which personal experience was the most shocking, each woman trying to win exclusive grieving rights to a particular topic.

During these get-togethers, the women would play a bizarre game called Sin-onyms. A specific sin would be read from a card, and each person would have a turn to cry out in grief and indignation while uttering an epithet that described the offense.

The competition was fierce. Beginners would opt for a simple "sad," "foul," "awful," "vile," or "disgraceful." Not to be outdone, intermediate players would up the ante with more descriptive words like "distressing," "ghastly," "horrendous," "repellent," or "loathsome." Scoffing at these single-word attempts, advanced players would choose phrases like "dreadfully appalling," "wretchedly abysmal," "monstrously abhorrent," "quite unspeakably repugnant," "most frightfully revolting," and "hideously, atrociously odious." The winner of the game would be granted a sobbing solo during the next Grievathon event.

The women even made up a song—a theme song, as it were, for their group parties. The song was sung to the tune of a haunting dirge and went like this:

We are the Grievers; we grieve day and night
For clothes that are either too short or too tight.
For necklines, and hemlines, and shirts with no sleeve,
We grieve.
Blouses that cling and that show off some cleavage—
These evils provide ample cause for more grievage;
Men with their V-necks that sport so much meavage*
And shorts that are so short you wouldn't believage!
We grieve, we grieve, we grieve.
We are the Grievers; we grieve night and day
For fabrics that are just a little too gay.
For colors worn proudly by heathens named Steve,
We grieve.

*meavage = man cleavage

There were many more stanzas covering other topics, such as music, but I don't recall them. Suffice it to say that I made it a point to steer clear of Madame Stringent and the Grievers as much as I could. I figured it would only be a matter of time before one of them found something wrong with me.

π π π π π

It wasn't long before preparations for the voyage to Hob were complete and I was summoned by the Queen to get ready for the journey. We convened in a large hall at the far end of the SPFGS. This, I was told, was the aviation center, where all the aircraft maintenance and testing took place. It was a large echoing space, with a concrete floor and multiple sliding panels built into the walls and ceiling. In one corner of the hall sat the Queen's private jet. I knew it was hers because the sparkly purple paint coating the vessel perfectly matched her flowing cape.

The hall was mostly empty otherwise, but, at one end, a large translucent panel stood, dividing the room into another section. On the other side of the dark panel loomed a large object. I could detect shapes and shadows through the semitransparent divider but couldn't determine what the massive thing was.

My curiosity was interrupted by the arrival of Qarl and Bobby, along with a few other humans and aliens that I assumed were staff or crew of some kind. We were directed to a long conference table set up in the middle of the hall, where we all seated ourselves while itinerary packets were handed out to us by a short, furry little fellow with 19 hands.

The packets were quite nicely put together: each was leather bound, with the title "Our Perilous Journey to Hob" printed in gold lettering on the front. I was beginning to thumb through my copy when I heard the Queen clear her throat.

"Let us begin the meeting," she purred, rising from her place at the head of the table. Her glowing breasts cast a gentle aura over our group, and her purple cape scintillated in the light. "We have much to talk about before we set forth on our journey. Does everyone have an itinerary?" Everybody at the table nodded. "Very well," she resumed. "Please open to page 1. The first item of business that must be discussed is—"

Here she was interrupted by the door at the end of the hall banging open. Everyone turned in their chairs at once to see what was going on. In swept Madame Stringent, flanked on either side by her two cohorts, Greta and Gretchen. They approached the table in long strides, halted, and bowed to the Queen, who raised one eyebrow at this unexpected intrusion. Qarl, who was sitting across from me, rolled his eyes and snickered.

"Your Majesty, I do apologize," began Madame Stringent in an urgent voice, "but a most grievous act has been committed that you must know about."

Greta and Gretchen nodded in agreement but kept their eyes averted. I couldn't tell if their downturned gazes were out of deference, fear, or discomfort at being so close to nudity, something their conservative selves generally preferred not to see.

Unperturbed, the Queen responded to Madame Stringent. "And what, pray tell, is this grievous act that has occurred?" she asked softly in an even voice.

"A murder, Your Grace. A murder!" Madame Stringent replied dramatically. Turning around to face us all, she widened her eyes as she announced to the table, "Somebody has killed Wonder Wasp!"

Everyone at the table collectively gasped at the news. I turned pale and tried to sink into my chair while Bobby bolted from his.

"Killed!?!" he exclaimed. "I wondered why I hadn't seen him in a few days. What happened?"

"We just discovered his body. It was most brutal the way it happened," replied Madame Stringent. "He was *crushed* to death!"

She pounded her fist onto the table as she screeched this, and everyone jumped (except the Queen, of course, who maintained her regal comportment and remained standing calmly with an inscrutable expression on her face). Bobby sat back down and waited for Madame Stringent to resume.

"Now then," she continued, dropping her voice to its characteristic chilly tone, "the question is who. Who committed this *terrible* and most *grievous* crime?" She punctuated the adjectives with dour seriousness.

My sweaty palms gripped the chair as Madame Stringent's hawkish gaze began roving the table, seeking answers. I knew that if her eyes locked onto me, she'd know the truth.

Everyone at the table turned to each other and began murmuring amongst themselves, puzzled over this unexpected turn of events. I sat there frozen, unsure of what to do. If I confessed to the killing, who knew what would happen to me? But if I didn't, I was confident that Madame Stringent would uncover my culpability sooner or later, and through methods I wasn't eager to discover. Dare I risk an unknown punishment by coming clean? Dare I risk Madame Stringent's hounding judgment by staying silent? In a split-second moment of decision, I rose suddenly from my chair.

"It was me!" I blurted out before I could stop myself. As soon as the words left my mouth, a hot flush came over me as I realized that there was no taking them back now. Trembling slightly, I fixed my gaze into the distance and announced to no one in particular, "I killed Wonder Wasp!"

The table collectively gasped again at this sudden development as all eyes turned and fixed upon me. The room fell silent, deathly silent. Not a finger stirred or a cape rustled. My pulse seemed like the loudest thing in the hall…thudding, thudding, thudding.

It was several long seconds before I finally retrieved the courage to break my distant gaze and look around the table. I wasn't assured by what I saw. Everyone sat with mouths open, staring at me with shocked expressions frozen on their faces—all except Madame Stringent, that is, who crouched, silently grieving, in the corner.

After a few seconds of tense, awful silence (during which I feared that Qarl's eyes would pop out of his head), the Queen leaned forward. "Why did you kill the Prophet?" she enquired gently.

"It was unintentional," I explained earnestly. "I mean, I meant to kill whatever it was, but I thought it was just an annoying bug." I hung my head. "I truly didn't mean to murder your Wonder Wasp." I stole a sideways glance at Bobby, wondering how he was taking this horrific news. To my surprise, he just shrugged.

"Don't worry about it," he said indifferently. "It happens. It was clearly an accident."

I was stunned at his unexpected flippancy. "Um…you aren't upset?" I asked tentatively. He flashed me an assuring smile.

"Nah, wasps die all the time. Even prophets like Wonder Wasp. There are plenty more of his breed around. It's no big deal."

I caught the Queen's eye, and she smiled slightly, affirming Bobby's reassurance to me. I sank back into my chair, trembling but relieved. *Whew, that was a close one!* I thought. My mind was still in partial disbelief, but my pulse gradually began to slow to its normal pace as my body realized that the worst was over.

With the mystery now solved, the Queen dismissed Madame Stringent, who reluctantly exited the hall with her sidekicks, glaring at me coldly as she swept past my chair. Once that interruption was out of the way, the Queen resumed the meeting, telling us all to turn to our packets once more as she began detailing the particulars of our impending expedition.

After about an hour of logistical discussion, much of which I didn't understand in the slightest, the Queen began wrapping up the meeting. She asked if anyone present had any questions, and a hand at the far end of the table went up. It belonged to a tall, thin alien, a green fellow with two heads, one of which was bald. It was the bald head that spoke.

"Your Immaculate Majesticness, we haven't discussed much the potential peril of this trip. What might happen if the Great Leaders of Hob become angry at our requests? Have we forgotten about...It?" A gasp went up from the table as he said this last part. The Queen raised her hand to silence the group.

"We are all fully aware of 'It,'" she said firmly. "It is a risk we must chance if we are to save our world. No one said this journey would be easy or without danger, but we cannot live our entire existence in perpetual fear of 'It.'"

What the hell is "It"? I thought curiously. I tried to catch Qarl's attention to ask, but the Queen was changing the subject.

"And now, I would like to introduce our new spacecraft pilot, who will be flying our crew to Hob. His name is Gurgatron, and he runs the finest space pilot academy on X@X. I have complete confidence that he will transport us to our destination safely. Gurgatron, would you like to say a few words?"

She stepped aside as Gurgatron rose clumsily from his place near the head of the table. He was a short, heavyset alien, shaped rather like a big brown egg. His narrow eyes sat far apart from each other on either side of his thick nose. His long arms and stumpy legs were covered with lumps, and his crusty brown skin had more folds than an accordion. I wouldn't have been surprised if his parents had turned out to be a potato and a toad.

Gurgatron lumbered eagerly to the head of the table and faced the group, his thick lips forming a serious pout.

"'Tis not to be an easy journey, folks," he grunted in a deep, raspy voice. "You'd best be prepared to stare danger in the eye and laugh. Indeed, I've encountered peril so many times in my travels that she's almost a friend to me." He chuckled heartily at his attempt at humor, but no one else laughed.

Resuming his sour expression, he continued. "There'll be no room on the ship for cowards, folks. If you're planning on bringing cowardice aboard my craft, I suggest you stay behind," he declared, pointing a fat finger at the group.

"Thank you, Gurgatron," the Queen interjected, taking her place once more at the head of the table while Gurgatron reseated himself reluctantly. "And now, I wish to show you all the great spacecraft that I had commissioned for just this occasion. It is the most technologically advanced ship of its kind, and if any craft can take us smoothly and safely to Hob, it can."

With that, she abruptly turned round and faced the translucent panel at the end of the hall. She clapped her hands together loudly, and the panel responded by dividing in the middle and folding itself into the walls on either side, revealing the giant object behind it.

"This, my friends," said the Queen proudly, gesturing grandly with her hand, "is the *Empress Galaqtica,* so named for its unique galaqtagon shape. No other ship in the universe has this groundbreaking design."

She was right. I had never seen anything quite like the *Empress Galaqtica*. A galaqtagon is a unique shape unlike any I have encountered on Earth, full of strange angles and corners. The ship was covered with 72 panels, and out of each one sprouted a winglike fin that could rotate at the pilot's discretion. A row of windows stretched around the ship, and the entire outer shell was painted a sparkling purple, perfectly matching the Queen's cape and her private jet. It was truly a beautiful ship.

"And now," the Queen concluded, wrapping up the meeting at last, "I want you all to begin your final preparations for our voyage. I wish to take off the moment everything is ready. You are all dismissed."

The hall became animated as everyone rose from their places and began scurrying to their duties. The Queen turned to me as I began to leave the table. "You, Qarl, and Bobby, come with me," she directed. "They will let us know when the ship is ready to board."

As we left the hall, I turned my head to steal one more look at the great ship that was to carry our little group on such a momentous journey. There was a nervous knot in my stomach. I didn't know what to expect on this trip, nor how I was ever going to convince two giant aliens to spare this planet, but one thing I did know: once I stepped onto the *Empress Galaqtica,* there was no going back.

Chapter F

Hmmmmmmmmmm. The low hum of the aircraft's engines vibrated my chair gently as I strapped myself into my seat in preparation for takeoff. I forced myself to breathe evenly, but I was truly nervous. Beside me, Bobby buckled himself in carefully. He seemed unfazed, but I wondered if, secretly, he was nervous too. After all, this voyage had the potential to change all of our lives…irrevocably.

Across the tiny aisle, Qarl had already strapped himself in. He gazed longingly at the cockpit door, his legs swinging in excitement. I knew he was absolutely thrilled with the ship and all of its state-of-the-art technology. Having lost his precious Ken.10 so recently, he had to have been going through withdrawals, and being on board such a splendid craft was his fix.

The Queen glided past our seats, ensuring everyone was fastened in safely before heading up to the cockpit to make last-mirkron checks with Gurgatron. I had been rather surprised when I found out that she was taking this journey with us. Being the Queen of the Cosmos, she was a valuable entity, and I thought it rather reckless of her to be taking part in such a dangerous mission involving extremely unpredictable results. But she had insisted that her presence was necessary, and so I dared not question her.

All told, there were 19 of us making the journey: the Queen, Qarl, Bobby, Gurgatron, the copilot Tippers, the first mate Quadrell, six alien members of the *Empress*'s crew, six human members of the Queen's military (three male and three female), and yours truly. It was an eclectic bunch, one that was sure to bring variety to the trip.

Tippers was the lone human member of the *Empress*'s crew. A spunky young woman, she had proven herself as one of the brightest and most skilled space pilots in the region. I learned from Bobby that she was one of the youngest pilots to ever pass through the Academy. She had been personally selected by Gurgatron to help helm the brand-new ship and transport us all safely to Hob. From the first confident, toothy smile she flashed at me during her preflight check, I knew that I was going to get along splendidly with her.

Quadrell was a tall and muscular alien. Quiet and thoughtful, he kept to himself and rarely spoke more than a few words at a time. He was a bi-planetary alien, his mother and father hailing from two different planets, so he had a distinctive look different from any other alien I had seen.

His skin was smooth and dark, and the only extra limb he possessed was a retractable tail. His arms and legs were thick and muscular, while his neck was thin and slender. He had two sets of eyes, one in the front and one in the back of his sphere-shaped head. The front pair were strong, masculine, and determined. The rear pair were soft, feminine, and gentle.

The most fascinating thing about Quadrell's unique appearance, however, was the whites of his eyes, which changed color to reflect his mood. Right now, they were a soft pink, which I interpreted as calm anticipation of the journey ahead. Despite his silent and serious demeanor, I found those eyes fascinating and very telling of the creature beneath the skin.

A voice crackled over the ship's intercom: it was Gurgatron. "Well, folks, fasten your seatbelts," he instructed, his deep voice thick with excitement. "We're ready for takeoff!"

I checked my belt one last time and leaned back in my seat. The engines beneath us began to hum louder as the *Empress Galaqtica* started to inch forward, heading toward the paneled wall at the end of the hall. A moment later, the wall divided in two, each side sliding back into recessed compartments to make way for the mighty ship. The aircraft glided through the opening and into the bright outdoors.

I peered out the large window next to my seat. Off to the side, I could see a long, straight runway that stretched off into the distance, beyond the grounds of the SPFGS and into the countryside, until it ended abruptly somewhere on the horizon.

The *Empress* continued to taxi, turning slowly until it had positioned itself at the start of the extensive airstrip. The engines idled as the ship paused momentarily…then came roaring to life as the *Empress Galaqtica* surged forward, picking up speed as it charged down the massive runway.

Pushed back in my seat by the force, I kept my head facing the window and watched the scenery whiz by faster and faster. It wasn't long before we had crossed the outer limits of the SPFGS and were making our way across the rest of the planet, hurtling toward the horizon down the long gray road.

A flash of white and blue caught my eye. We were passing by the Gerfron's homestead. His dilapidated house perched sadly on top of its small snowy hill, surrounded by a sea of his blue Shonkleshorn sheep. I caught a glimpse of him outside juicing one of his sheep, and I think he waved as we raced by.

The Frobo-Zo-Polo's house was the next one we passed. His place was decorated in bright yellows, and he had set up a small yo-yo stand in his front yard, the perfect expression of his singular hobby. Above the stand hung a large sign. I strained to read the black lettering, which blurred as we whizzed by: **Yo-yos sold here. Best haggle in town! ONLY ONE MAY BE BOUNCED AT A TIME!!!**

We continued down the runway at a rapid pace, the *Empress Galaqtica* soon reaching breakneck speed. I was bracing myself for what I anticipated would be imminent liftoff when, over the roar of the engines, I heard the tinkling of bells. We were nearing the home of the Frapalapper, the singing cave creature who lived near the edge of X@X. And that's when I was hit with a terrifying realization.

"Bobby!" I exclaimed, turning in my seat to face him. "We're going to drive right off the edge of the planet, aren't we!"

"Of course," he replied calmly, looking up from the magazine he had been reading. "Our planet isn't round, like yours. There's no need for any sort of perpendicular liftoff. So why not just soar off the edge of the wedge and out into space?"

"But—but is that safe?" I sputtered. I couldn't help but picture this scenario not being unlike driving a car off a cliff. Beyond the window I could hear a high-pitched singing voice intermingling with the clanging bells. The Frapalapper's cave was getting closer, and with it, the edge of X@X.

"It's perfectly safe," Bobby assured me, "if you have enough speed. Of course, there is always the chance that the craft won't have enough momentum to break through the atmosphere. If that were to happen, X@X's gravitational pull would take hold of us the moment we dropped off the edge, whipping us around and smashing us into the underside of the planet. But that won't happen. Gurgatron is the best pilot around. Don't worry."

I gulped. I *was* worried. My heart rate increased as adrenaline pumped through my body. The Frapalapper's song rose in pitch and volume, flooding my ears with its haunting, dissonant melody—an omen of doom, perhaps?

Outside our windows I could see the edge of the planet approaching quickly. The colorful land stretched out on either side of our craft like the edge of a beach, while the blue sky closed in like waves about to crash over us.

The *Empress* drove faster and faster, its wheels vibrating over the paved runway. The engines squealed louder, their metallic tones clashing with the Frapalapper's song. The world outside flashed by in ribbons of smeared color. Sight and sound overwhelmed my senses as the massive sea of blue loomed closer and closer until it was almost upon us. I was certain that we were about to die.

And then, in an instant, the solid ground under our ship gave way to intangible sky. I let out an involuntary gasp. The sound of the rumbling wheels ceased abruptly, and the Frapalapper's tones faded into the distance behind us as any signs of land disappeared from my field of view. For a moment, I felt suspended in space and time, surrounded by misty blue above me, below me, and around me. Only the engine's roar remained constant as I held my breath, unsure of whether I was flying, falling, or floating.

As if in slow motion, I turned my head and looked around the cabin. Bobby sat with his eyes fixed on his magazine. Across the aisle, Qarl perched on his seat excitedly, his purple lips stretched into a massive grin, his large eyes reflecting the bright blue outside his window. In her place by the cockpit, the Queen rested calmly with eyes closed, her purple cape wrapped around her and glittering in the bright light that streamed through the cabin.

Slowly I turned my head once more to face the sea of sky outside my window, the engines still roaring in my ears. My pulse continued to race as we remained suspended in this nothingness. I waited with bated breath for a resolution to this tension, gripping the armrests of my chair in a subconscious attempt to grab hold of some reality.

Then, before I could blink, the view outside my window changed. The misty sea of blue instantly became an ocean of black dotted with bright stars and colorful planets. We had broken through the atmosphere! We were safely in space now, away from the deadly pull of X@X.

I settled back in my chair with a relieved sigh, letting out a silent cheer, while the rest of the cabin appeared remarkably calm. Behind us, X@X grew smaller and smaller until it was only a tiny wedge in our trail.

Gurgatron turned off the seatbelt sign, and a few of our party got up to move around a bit. As soon as his sign de-illuminated, Qarl hopped off his seat and headed over to pester Quadrell about the various nuances of the ship. The Queen entered the cockpit to check on Gurgatron and Tippers while Bobby went to go use the restroom.

With nothing in particular to do, I took to eavesdropping on the two aliens in the row behind mine. They were laughing heartily, regaling each other with various jokes (such as why the chicken crossed the Andromeda Galaxy, what you get if you cross a Zurkmeister with a Krippit, or how many dolgogs it takes to change a hyperspace illumination capsule).

I was just about to interject with a space-themed joke of my own when my attention was distracted by the Queen exiting the cockpit. She stopped Quadrell, who was just coming up the aisle, Qarl trailing behind him. The trio halted a few feet from my seat.

"Quadrell, I just spoke with the captain, and we are very close to entering Middle Space," the Queen told him. "Is the gas ready?"

Quadrell nodded silently, and the Queen returned to her seat by the cockpit. Qarl and the first mate continued up the aisle, and I grabbed Qarl's arm as he passed by me.

"Qarl!" I hissed, keeping my voice low. "Come here." I pulled him out of the aisle, and he plopped into Bobby's seat, his face betraying how irked he was at the interruption.

"What do you want?" he huffed. "I was just about to watch Quadrell check some meters."

"Give it a rest, buddy," I cautioned. "Can't you tell that he's getting a little annoyed with you following him around? His eyes were turning orange."

Qarl shrugged defiantly. "I don't care. This is too cool of an opportunity to pass up. The ship is incredible!" His eyes widened as he spoke. "Makes me wonder how my poor Ken.10 is doing. You know, the tube that you helped ruin." He looked at me pointedly. "The Queen isn't too thrilled, by the way, that the brand new teletransportube she got for me is gone already. She said she won't be able to get me another one for a while." His big lips turned into a pout.

I held up my hands. "Knock off the drama, Qarl," I scolded him. "I didn't stop you to talk about this. I wanted to ask you about what the Queen was telling Quadrell."

Qarl's face contorted with displeasure at the prospect of having to answer more of my questions. "What's to know?

You were in the meeting earlier. We have to pass through Middle Space to get to Hob."

"Middle Space?" I questioned.

"Yes, Middle Space," he repeated, mimicking my voice sarcastically. "Didn't you take Madame Stringent's science class? You should know this."

My blank stare was not reassuring.

"Ugh, fine. I suppose I'll explain...again," Qarl said, rolling his eyes and leaning back in Bobby's seat with a huff. "But pay attention this time!"

I nodded, and Qarl continued. "Space is divided into three sections. The inner section is Confined Space, where your Solar System resides. X@X rests right on the edge of Confined Space. Then there's Middle Space, which we're heading into now. It's the largest of the three sections, and it's full of many different planets and aliens. Not too many Humans though."

"So what's the third section?" I asked.

"Hyper Space. That's the outermost section of the Universe," he explained. "Residents of Hyper Space tend to be...well, hyper. Very active and energetic. Most planet builders live there. It's also where Hob is, which is where we're going, in case you hadn't paid attention."

I chose to ignore this last remark. "So what's this gas the Queen was talking about?"

"Didn't you listen at all in the meeting?" Qarl asked incredulously. "It's in the itinerary. We're making a stop to drop gas on some parts of Middle Space."

"I suppose you know what my next question is, then," I remarked with a smirk.

"Unfortunately, I do," Qarl sighed. "You want to know why."

I nodded, and he reluctantly continued. "Middle Space is a vast area containing multiple pockets of isolated unrest. There are some planets—like Qari and Nari—that have been bickering and warring with each other for as long as we can recall. The violence rarely spills over into other areas, but the Queen wishes to keep peace in the Universe as much as possible. So, every once in a while, one of her pilots flies over and drops CO gas on the fighting planets."

"They drop carbon monoxide on them?" I asked, horrified.

"No, stupid. Chill-Out gas," Qarl countered. "It's a powerful gas that mellows the aliens out and makes them think peaceful and happy thoughts. Also makes them a bit sleepy." He chuckled. Leaning closer, he dropped his voice to a whisper. "A few of us on X@X use the stuff recreationally, but don't tell anyone!"

"You're crazy, Qarl. You know that?" I told him, shaking my head.

He shrugged. "No crazier than anyone else. Hey, listen. I'm going to go with Quadrell when he gets ready to drop the gas. I might be able to sneak you a vial of it if you want to try it." His face was glowing with excitement, undoubtedly at the tantalizing prospect of getting me buzzed, but I shook my head.

"Qarl, there's no way in space that I'm going to start huffing recreational gas with you."

His face morphed into a disappointed expression. "You're such a lame Human," he muttered. Spotting Bobby returning from the bathroom, he hopped off the seat and stepped into the aisle. "I'll see you later," he called back at me as he moseyed to the front of the cabin in search of Quadrell.

Bobby sat back down. "Have we dropped the gas yet?" he asked me, picking up his magazine.

"Apparently, we're about to," I replied. After hesitating a moment, I turned to my seatmate. "Say, Bobby…have you ever…tried chill-out gas?"

Bobby threw back his head and laughed. "I did a couple times," he replied. "But it made me interpret prophecies in very weird ways. After a few scary interpretations, I decided it wasn't for me. Sure seems to work well on some of those planets though…at least until it wears off. Then they're right back to fighting."

With that, Bobby returned to his magazine, and I returned my gaze to the window. Outside, colorful planets floated slowly by, while stars shone brightly in the distance against the deep blackness of space. Occasionally a comet or asteroid would streak past, reminding me once more of the two great aliens of Hob and their games. I wondered what they would be like when I finally met them. *How big are they? Will they be fearsome? Will they listen to me? Will they try to hurt me? What if I can't convince them to spare X@X?*

My chaotic thoughts were interrupted by the sound of snoring. I glanced over at Bobby; he had fallen asleep in his seat, the magazine still open in his lap. And wouldn't you know, it was a home improvement magazine. *Well that makes sense,* I thought wryly.

Turning back to the window, I was startled by a long blue arm thrusting a vial under my nose. I jerked back with a little gasp. Qarl popped his head up from behind the seat in front of me, a mischievous grin on his face.

"Gotcha!" he whispered in triumph.

"Qarl!" I hissed at him. "Just what do you think you're doing!?!"

"Giving you the best ride of your life," he responded. "I was able to get some CO gas when Quadrell wasn't looking."

"Well, I am *not* going to try any, so you can just forget it!" I whispered defiantly.

"Too late," he replied. "It only takes a whiff, and your shocked snort was more than sufficient. How do you feel?" he asked with a smile.

I was starting to feel a bit drowsy, but I fought the sensation. "I am feeling just fine," I insisted. "Just…fine."

My struggle against the powerful gas was futile, however. I could feel my heart rate beginning to slow as my muscles proceeded to relax one by one until I was melting into my seat. I felt a stupid grin forming on my face, even while I tried to stop it. My anxious thoughts disappeared into misty crevices of my brain as I settled into a peaceful, euphoric state.

"Qarl, wut's haaaapppppennniinng?" I slurred, barely able to summon enough energy for my lips to form the words.

"It's ok…ok…ok…" his voice echoed in my ears. "Just relax…relax…relax…"

My eyelids grew heavy as my mind was overtaken with pleasant thoughts. I was flying effortlessly through space, on such a happy adventure, with all my best friends around me. We were all having such a grand, wonderful party. I knew Asdf and Jkl would totally love to party with us. Boy, this gas was awesome.

"Qarllll, you're my besssst friennnnnd…" I managed to slur. I was feeling so sleepy, yet so happy.

"I knoooooow…" was the last thing I heard before drifting off into a deep sleep.

Chapter G

"WAKE UP! HEY. HEY! HELLO? WAKE UP!"

A distant voice invaded my subconscious as I felt myself being pulled out of my peaceful, foggy slumber. I was being shaken by some powerful force. Reluctantly opening one eye, I saw a blurry blue blob standing over me. I blinked slowly a few times to clear my vision. Qarl had me by the shoulders and was shaking me.

"Dude, wake up already!"

I tried to shake the haze out of my head as my brain was slowly becoming aware of where I was. "W-what happened?" I stuttered. "How long was I out?"

"Long enough," Qarl replied. "We've landed already."

I bolted upright in my seat and scanned the cabin. It was empty except for Qarl and me. "We've reached Hob already?" I asked, fumbling nervously with my seatbelt.

"No, silly," Qarl replied with an eye-roll. "We've stopped on Xoqdo. It's a small asteroid fueling station."

I glanced out my window. We had indeed stopped on a dark planetary body. The terrain was rocky and gray, and not a building or a living creature was to be seen. We seemed to be the only signs of civilization there.

Qarl motioned for me to follow him, and I staggered out of my seat, still feeling the aftereffects of the CO gas. We stepped out of the *Empress Galaqtica* and onto the jagged terrain of Xoqdo. As soon as my foot touched the surface, a cold chill hit me in the face, sending shivers through my entire body. Above our heads, the blackness of space hovered menacingly, the glowing stars staring down on us like evil eyes.

We circled around to the back of the ship, where the rest of our party stood huddled around a large rickety pump, which was vibrating violently. A long hose connected the pump to a fixture on the underside of the *Empress*.

Qarl explained that the fueling station was connected to a deep underground drill that mined for zog, a special mineral commonly used to fuel spacecraft. Asteroids like Xoqdo were unsuitable to live on due to their harsh terrain and severe weather, but because they were often rich in minerals like zog, they made for very convenient fueling stations scattered throughout space.

Qarl and I joined the group circled around the pump. Gurgatron was fiddling with the control pad next to it, a frustrated look on his gruff face. A few of the alien crew inspected the hose for kinks while Tippers and Quadrell examined the pump itself. Meanwhile, the members of the Queen's military had set up a perimeter around our landing site, keeping a sharp lookout for anything hostile.

I shivered in the cold air. Beside me, Bobby rubbed his hands together to keep warm as he looked anxiously at the fueling operation in progress. Even the Queen had her cape wrapped snugly about her against the bitter chill. She stood next to the control pad with Gurgatron, watching the proceedings calmly.

"I'm afraid this pump is about dry, Your Majesty," Gurgatron informed the Queen grimly. "It's bringing up zog all right, but only a bit at a time. At this pace, fueling will take all night."

"What are our options, Gurgatron?" the Queen asked. The heavyset sky skipper scratched his lumpy head.

"Well, ma'am, we can take off again and try to find another fueling station, but there's no telling when we'll run into another one. You know how unpredictable these asteroid patterns can be, especially with how much They like to play with them."

The Queen nodded knowingly. "And if we stay here?"

"Well, we could sit tight here all night, I suppose," Gurgatron considered. "It'd be cold as fuck—excuse my language, ma'am—but we'd be fully fueled and ready to take off at first light." He folded his long arms behind his back, stealing a sheepish glance up at the Queen, but she didn't even raise an eyebrow at his vulgar slip-up.

"We shall camp here, then," she decided.

π π π π π

After a bland but nutritious dinner of nebula shakes, our party retired to the *Empress*'s sleeping quarters for bed. The six military personnel were placed on guard duty rotation, two at a time. They patrolled around our campsite, bundled up tight against the frigid air. The Queen and Gurgatron each had their own private room, while the rest of us were divvied up into the other compartments. The alien crew members piled onto two sets of triple bunks, leaving five of us to pair off into the remaining double bunks.

Tippers had intended to share a bunk bed with Quadrell, who had gone to sleep the instant he was dismissed, but Qarl had already claimed that spot. I swear that little blue alien didn't intend to let Quadrell out of his sight the entire trip. For me, I selected a lounge chair in a corner by one of the windows. I wanted a break from bunk beds after enduring them during the college semester.

"I guess that leaves you and me, then," Tippers told Bobby cheerfully. Bobby flushed slightly.

"Yeah, guess so," he replied, attempting a confident grin but avoiding eye contact.

With everyone in their respective sleeping spots at last, lights were dimmed, and the ship grew silent. Snug in my chair, I pulled a blanket over myself and closed my eyes. Despite my long nap earlier, I was still feeling a bit drowsy from the lingering effects of the gas, so it wasn't long before I once again drifted off into the realm of dreams.

I was just sinking into the mysterious depths of my subconscious, the opening images of a dream beginning to flash across my mind, when my senses became suffused with a deep pink glow. Swirling mists appeared and began surrounding me slowly, creeping through my mind like an inescapable fog. The dream images began to flicker, and I saw the inside of the ship once again, bathed in a soft reddish-pink that seemed to grow brighter with each second.

As the mists encircled me, I found myself floating up above my body, looking down at it sleeping in the chair, eyes still closed. Staring down at my resting form, I watched in surreal wonder as the curling mists wrapped around it like witchy fingers, pulling my body effortlessly forward and carrying it as if with ghostly hands.

I gazed, transfixed, as my body drifted through the cabin and out into the night. In a daze, I followed, drawn by the wispy fog and the soft, pink light that beckoned me from just beyond the rocks ahead.

As I continued watching in a trancelike vision, I saw two bright points of light appear in the pink glow before me. They glided toward my floating body, growing brighter and larger as they approached. They reminded me of the Queen's two shining nipples, beaming with a pulsating gleam and oh-so-inviting. My body moved closer to the enchanting light, arms outstretched to embrace it. The mists continued to dance dreamily, catching the pink glow and refracting it in all directions.

Then, before my eyes, a dark horse emerged slowly from the bewitching haze. She was a beautiful mare, tall and smooth, her flowing mane wisping in a dreamlike slow motion. Her edges were fluid and undefined, making her appear like a dark apparition floating through the rosy brume. The twin luminescent beams were her eyes, and they bathed my body with their cool pink light as she approached slowly, majestically, her hooves never touching the ground.

My mind began to feel thick and cloudy as the mare neared my body, the pink light growing ever stronger. I felt drowsy, hypnotized. Flashes of black appeared in my vision as the scene unfolding before me quivered and blurred. I began to see glimpses of past dreams; they passed before my mind's eye at a frenetic pace, intermingling with the visions I was now witnessing.

The mists began to ensnare my senses more aggressively, obscuring my thoughts and sight. Through the densely growing fog, I saw my body collapse to the ground. Something was wrong. Pushing against the invading mists in desperation, I cried out.

In a flash, I felt myself being pulled downward and into my body again. My eyes flew open as if I had been startled from sleep. *What just happened? Have I been dreaming?*

I was staring up at black sky and felt cold, hard ground beneath my back. Out of the corner of my eye I could see the ship looming in the distance, dark and silent. The military guards were nowhere in sight.

Before I could wonder how I had gotten from being curled up in my cozy chair to lying on the rocky ground outside, I was blinded by a pair of pink lights shining in my face. It was the dark horse; she was standing over me and staring down into my eyes, her own sending a piercing light that reached into my soul.

I was paralyzed. I couldn't escape her crippling gaze as the bright light entered me and wrapped itself around my innermost senses. I was mesmerized yet terrified, wanting to escape even while I remained entranced by its power. Once again, my vision wavered as dreamlike images flashed across my mind.

I felt myself go numb as a powerful force seemed to pull me from this world and into another. I opened my mouth to call for help but couldn't hear myself cry out. My eyes fluttered…I was blacking out…

Suddenly, a purple glow washed over me, chasing all traces of pink away in a wave of relief. I felt myself released instantly from the pink light's gripping hold. Above me I saw the dark horse rear her head and stagger back from the purple onslaught. Rolling out from under her, I crawled to shelter behind a jagged rock. I peered out from behind it and was amazed at what I saw.

The Queen was standing where I had lain only moments before, her profile tall and majestic against the black night. Her cape flowed grandly behind her, sparkling within a purple halo that surrounded her entire being.

But what amazed me the most were her breasts. What had before been two soft pale lights radiating gently from her nipples were now two torrents of purple light streaming out from her body. Her nipples had become weapons as energy coursed from them like swirling lasers, connecting with the mare's pink glow and enveloping it slowly in magnificent purple.

As I watched in speechless wonder, the horse staggered back bit by bit, her bold pink eyes fading into a faint glimmer as her glow grew weaker and weaker under the crushing purple. The Queen continued forward, step by step, unrelenting, her smooth skin shining in the light.

The next instant, all vestiges of pink vanished from the night. The purple streams reversed their direction and retreated into the Queen's body, leaving only the nipples shining with a residual radiance. The dark mare's eyes blackened, and, as I watched in fearful awe, she vaporized into a shapeless dark mass that drifted off into the shadows, not to be seen again. The purple halo surrounding the Queen slowly faded away, and the light from her breasts returned to its warm, familiar glow.

Shaking, I picked myself up off the ground and tentatively emerged from behind my rock. Upon spotting me, the Queen swept over and took my hand, guiding me to a large smooth stone, where she sat me down to rest.

"Are you all right?" she asked earnestly, bending down and scanning my face with her beautiful eyes.

"Y-yes, I think so," I stuttered, still feeling weak from the ordeal. "What happened to me? What was that thing?"

The Queen stepped back and seated herself on a small rocky ledge across from me, wrapping her cape about her as she replied.

"That was the Night Mare."

"What was she trying to do to me?"

"She was attempting to invade your dreams. She is a dream killer."

I shook my head, trying to snap my mind from its flummoxed fog. "What's a dream killer?"

"They are creatures that have the power to invade people's minds and use that power to do so during their dreams," she explained. "Dream killing is a dark magic that is strictly forbidden to use, but there are those that do."

"Why would someone invade a dream?"

"Usually with the intent of destroying it."

"But what would be the point of that? They're just dreams…aren't they?"

The Queen shook her head. "Not entirely. There are people among those who study magic—myself included—who believe that dreams are more than merely the resting mind's fancies…that dreams, in fact, can be portals to alternate realities." My eyes widened at this.

"You see," she continued, "the mind often connects with other versions of itself in other dimensions during the safety of sleep. Dreams can become hallways or platforms across which the mind can enter another reality.

"However, when a dream is invaded, altered, or destroyed unnaturally, the bridging connection it provides becomes lost, and the dreamer may become trapped in one of these alternate realities—a reality they were never meant to live. This is why using mind magic to affect dreams is forbidden."

"But what motive would someone like the Night Mare have to mess with people's dreams in such a way?" I questioned, still confused. "Why would someone want to trap people in other realities?"

The Queen rose from the ledge and began to pace. "Each has her own reasons," she said, a faraway look in her eyes. "For the Night Mare, hers is a lust for power, a dangerous lust that has overtaken her and turned her magic into darkness. Killing dreams, and ultimately affecting others' realities, feeds her intense cravings for control and power. Any person who dreams is a potential victim of hers, a prey on which she can feed, a pawn whose destiny she can control. Thankfully, you were not fully asleep when she cast her spell, else you may not have been able to notice her, let alone resist her."

"I would've been a goner if you hadn't shown up," I replied gratefully. "I didn't know you had special powers like…that." I lowered my head and blushed, uncomfortable at discussing the Queen's beautiful body. She smiled down at me and resumed her place on the ledge.

"I'm not like any human you're familiar with," she purred softly. "I'm a space witch. I have powers that many other humans do not."

"Powers like the Night Mare?" I ventured cautiously. The Queen looked off into the distance. An uncomfortable pause followed.

"We share more magic than you know," she said finally, her soft voice barely perceptible as a wistful look came into her gentle eyes. "She is my sister."

Chapter H

My eyes almost popped out of my head at the Queen's revelation. *Did I hear her correctly?* I wondered incredulously. As if sensing my thoughts, the Queen repeated herself.

"Yes, the Night Mare is indeed my sister." She fixed her eyes once again on a point in the distance. "Long ago, she used to be a beautiful woman and a powerful space witch. We were quite close, she and I, and we intended to protect the cosmos together."

I nodded, leaning forward in rapt attention. The Queen took a slow, deep breath and continued. "Unfortunately, as I rose to power, she became jealous of the authority I had attained. As her hunger for control grew, she began to use her powers recklessly, crossing into dangerous magic in an attempt to gain an edge on me in ruling the universe."

"What happened then?" I asked breathlessly.

"Well, contrary to what some may think, I did not mind sharing rule of the universe with my sister. But she was becoming dangerous and began violating rules I had put into place to protect the residents of the cosmos. Despite my attempts at pleading with her, she only grew darker and darker. When she started to interfere with dreams, I knew I had to stop her."

The Queen's normally steady voice cracked slightly with emotion. "I did not wish to destroy her, for despite how much of a stranger she had become to me, she was still my sister, after all. Even in the face of her evil, I could not will myself to kill her, for love is a powerful magic all its own."

"So what did you do?" I asked.

The Queen faltered for a moment, then rose from her seat and stepped over to where the intense battle had taken place earlier that night. Turning to me with a sad expression I had never seen on her face before, she answered me with a pained voice.

"I cursed her. I turned her into a mare so that all she encountered would know her true form and intentions, and be forewarned. I then banished her to wander the night skies forever."

I sat up straight, struck with a sudden realization. "The Horsehead Nebula!" I exclaimed. "That's her!"

The Queen nodded soberly. "Yes, from your Earth she appears in the sky as the Horsehead Nebula. And to this day, though but a shadow of her former self, she continues to revel in her dark magic, the very magic that destroyed her."

"I guess I should consider myself lucky that I survived," I said, overwhelmed with feelings of awe and gratitude. "I definitely don't know what I would've done had you not shown up when you did."

The Queen smiled slightly and stepped over to me, taking my hand. "I am looking out for you. You are very important to this trip."

I rose from my stone and began walking with her back to the ship, a troubling question still nagging at my mind. "But why? Why am I so important to this trip? I know I was chosen by prophecy, and I understand that I'm from a planet that Asdf and Jkl like a lot, but—I mean—you're the Queen of the Cosmos! What makes you think the 'Great Leaders' would value my opinion so much more over yours?"

The Queen stopped and turned to me. "I cannot do this myself. Even being queen, I have my limitations."

"And what are those?" I pressed curiously.

The Queen paused a moment before continuing. "I didn't tell you this earlier, but you are bound to know sooner than later. The distrust I have toward the two leaders of Hob is mutual. They are not particularly fond of me."

"How come?" I wondered, confused. "I mean, you practically do all their hard work for them."

"They see me as a potential threat," she explained. "Aliens tend to be a fearful species, and when I rose to power, Asdf and Jkl kept a watchful eye on me. Being a human, I was a suspicious outsider to them, and I believe they were worried that I would rally my species and my planet to take the cosmos from them.

"When I cursed my sister, that was a turning point. They became convinced that I was intent on taking over the universe and usurping their position as head over all. In their view, a woman who is willing to curse her own sister to get ahead is a threat."

"I see," I replied.

"As time has passed, they have never confronted me, and I have tried to keep order and peace without encroaching on them either, but there is a definite tension between us. And now I fear that this purge they are planning may only be an excuse to get rid of X@X and me once and for all. I cannot be sure of that, but one thing is certain: any attempts by me to plead with them will be futile. I need you." She placed her hands on my shoulders and locked her mesmerizing eyes with mine. "I need you," she repeated softly.

I took in her gaze, marveling at its charm and power even as my mind filled with more questions. "But I am a human too," I said. "What makes you think Asdf and Jkl will trust me?"

The Queen removed her hands from my shoulders and began to pace in front of me. "You raise a fair question," she replied. "But there are differences between Earth-humans and other humans of the universe. Your kind lacks the powers that would seem threatening to Hob. Besides, Asdf and Jkl have a great respect for Earth. My trust is that this respect extends to its residents as well."

"And if it doesn't?"

"Then X@X has lost what may be its last hope."

I nodded, a lump in my throat. I was finally beginning to feel the full importance of my mission, and while it terrified me, it also empowered my being with a solemn sense of responsibility. X@X needed me, and I was going to be there to save it!

As we made our way back to the ship, I noticed the two guards crumpled up against the landing struts, sound asleep, their slumber an apparent side effect of the Night Mare's spell that had been cast around the area. As the Queen entered the *Empress Galaqtica* before me, I rushed over and shook them awake before their torpid lapse in duty could be noticed. Without missing a beat, I fell in line behind the Queen again as we stepped inside and proceeded back to the sleeping quarters, where she softly bade me goodnight and retired to her chamber.

Reclining back in my chair once more, I stared at the ceiling, my mind active with thoughts of the bizarre occurrences of the night. The enormity of my mission was beginning to settle upon my shoulders, and my anxiety threatened to kick in. I really felt far from home.

I didn't feel like going to sleep, considering what had happened the last time I had done so, but I knew that I had to get some rest before the morning. Glancing instinctively out the window for any signs of danger in the blackness, I was slightly reassured by the sight of the guards patrolling once more (although their yawns were less assuring).

Leaning back in my chair and pulling my blanket over me, I closed my eyes and attempted to quiet my mind. I was sure the morning would bring its own challenges.

π π π π π

By the next morning, the refueling process was complete, and Gurgatron wasted no time in getting us on our way again. The journey through Middle Space was long yet full of beautiful sights. I kept Qarl and Bobby busy answering my many questions. Bobby kept a patient smile on his face throughout, while Qarl, as was his nature, didn't bother to hide any of his annoyance.

Quadrell maintained his silent patrol through the interior, checking valves and dials and gauges as needed, while Tippers came back from the cockpit from time to time to update us on our progress. I noticed that Bobby seemed distracted from my questions whenever she was present.

The Queen kept her place at the front of the cabin, occasionally catching my eye and lifting the corners of her lips in a barely perceptible smile of assurance. After the dark events of the previous night, I felt safer knowing she was within sight. I truly was glad that she had insisted on accompanying our group to Hob.

After a time, Tippers emerged from the cockpit to announce that we were entering the Corridor, a region of space bounded on all sides by many beautiful and intriguing sights. She advised me to keep my eyes fixed outside the window so as not to miss anything. Qarl and Bobby moved closer to me, preparing to act as my "tour guides."

Beyond my window, celestial bodies passed by, each with its own characteristics and story to tell. There was Kapo, the perfectly round and smooth planet that looked like a giant shiny ball—no civilization or even terrain to be seen. Bobby explained to me that this seemingly deserted place was actually an inverse planet: all life lived inside the hollow sphere, a reverse gravity force grounding objects to the inside edges by pulling them outward—the opposite of how planets like X@X and Earth grounded objects by pulling them inward against the outside surface.

There was the group of polite planets, beacons of peaceful civility amidst the regions of turmoil scattered throughout Middle Space. The largest of these polite planets was Adanaq, where, I was told, frequent ceremonies were held to exchange pleasant trees and nice cities amongst the group.

There was Cudno, the strange galactic object that could not be clearly identified, a shapeless mass of intergalactic dust that traversed the cosmos, looking for love and acceptance.

There was Famm, a cluster of bodies that consisted of 72 meteoroid children orbiting their parent comet. The comet drifted wearily along the Corridor, its tail drooping, no doubt exhausted from caring for so many offspring. The meteoroids were rowdy things, bouncing into each other rambunctiously and occasionally escaping orbit, much to their parent's distress.

There was the Great Middle Space Asteroid Belt, which Qarl explained had previously encircled Middle Space but had mysteriously become unbuckled some time ago, leaving the belt to snake aimlessly across the region. The buckle was missing, and theories abounded as to its whereabouts.

"Some say it was stolen by Asdf and Jkl," Qarl told me. "Others say it became detached and drifted to the Edge of the Universe, lost forever. A few even speculate that it was ground down and used for fuel by a desperate rogue division of the Space Pilots Union. No one seems to know."

"Well, at least no one seems to have messed with Orion's Belt," I quipped.

Qarl looked at me strangely. "What are you talking about? Orion doesn't have a belt."

"Sure he does," I countered confidently. "Those bright stars in a row in the middle of the constellation. It's the Belt of Orion. Trust me, I learned it in school."

"Well then your school must be either ignorant or quite prudish," Qarl said with a chuckle. "That's Orion's penis."

"His what?"

"His penis. Orion's kind of a hotshot. He doesn't care too much for the 'guys can't show their bodies' rule. So he brazenly shows off his gigantic penis for all to see. It's kind of his 'fuq you' to the Universe."

"And what does the Queen think about this?"

"Eh, she's got bigger things to worry about. She tends to choose her battles carefully. Madame Stringent, though, has made it her life's mission to put an end to Orion's open display."

"And how does she intend to do that?" I wondered curiously.

"No idea," Qarl replied, shrugging. "She's always making a big deal out of things though. Like Wonder Wasp's death. She acts like she doesn't know that there are many other wasp prophets around who can take his place."

"Sounds like she's looking to create tension."

"She's a stickler for the rules and believes in harsh justice meted out immediately to any and all offenders. She has her own interpretation of the laws, and she's frequently at odds with the Queen, who is very careful with what she chooses to enforce or overlook."

"Like the nudity thing?" I ventured.

"That's one example," Qarl agreed. "The official law says no nudity for males. The Queen only tends to enforce that in her immediate region. She can't realistically be expected to patrol the entire Universe, prosecuting modesty offenders. Madame Stringent, on the other hand, not only wants complete rule enforcement far and wide, but insists that it is not appropriate for females to display their bodies either. You've seen how she and her sidekicks dress." He made a face at the thought of their fashion choices.

"The Queen must be a walking reminder to them of the openness of female nudity, then," I mused. "How irritating that must be for them." I chuckled, a bit delighted at the thought. My short experience with Madame Stringent and her cohorts had left me with an intense desire to see their pious attempts thwarted.

Suddenly, our conversation was interrupted by the sound of the engines sputtering. The lights in the cabin dimmed and flickered. Bobby stood up from his seat.

"What's going on?" he questioned, a look of concern etched onto his face. The words were barely out of his mouth when the *Empress Galaqtica* fell dark and silent. The engines ceased their sputtering, and the only light in the cabin emanated from the Queen's chest. The Queen rose from her seat and turned to enter the cockpit, but she was met by Tippers coming out.

"Tippers, is everything all right?" the Queen asked in a low but serious tone.

"We've lost all power to the ship," Tippers replied, her voice tense. "Gurgatron thinks a stray magnetic field from Hob has interfered with our electronics."

"Those blasted idiots!" Bobby blurted out. "Don't they realize how dangerous their 'playtime' can be for the rest of us?"

I looked over at Qarl. His blue face seemed pale in the darkness, and he remained silent.

"What about the backup generator?" the normally quiet Quadrell spoke up.

"That's fried as well," Tippers answered.

"What do we do?" I asked. The silence from the mighty ship was unnerving, and I could feel us beginning to descend.

"Gurgatron is trying to touch down on the nearby planet Fweam," Tippers replied. "Everyone, get in your seats and prepare for a rough landing." With that, she rejoined Gurgatron in the cockpit.

As we complied with Tippers' order, I felt a lump rising in my throat. I knew that, in our situation, "touching down" meant "crashing." Peering out the window, I could see a planet beneath us growing larger by the second. *That must be Fweam,* I thought, hoping Gurgatron would be able to find an ideal place on it to land the ship.

The cabin was quiet as everyone sat, contemplating our impending fate. Qarl stared straight ahead, an inscrutable expression on his pale face. Quadrell's eyes had turned yellow, glowing softly in the darkness as if to warn us of the danger we were in. Bobby pulled his cap low over his face; perhaps he was trying to hide his fear from the others or was attempting to shield himself from the grim reality he was trapped in. The Queen remained composed, but even she could not hide the fear that flashed in her gentle eyes.

As for me, I tried to keep my body as limp as possible—having read somewhere that this was an ideal way to limit injury in a crash scenario—but the tension that surged through my body was too much to overcome. The knot in the pit of my stomach tightened as I felt the aircraft continue to drop toward the ground.

Against my better judgment, I took one final look out the window. I could no longer see the horizon as my view became filled with the ground rushing up to meet us. My heart began to race. I closed my eyes, grabbed the armrests of my chair with my sweaty fingers, and braced for impact.

Chapter 1

The hideous screech of metal scraping rock filled the cabin, setting my teeth on edge and raising the hairs on the back of my neck. I gripped the armrests tighter, my nails digging into the luxurious leather, as the ship careened over the rocky terrain at a terrifying speed. Finally—an eternity later—we lurched to a stop. My head bounced against the back of the seat in front of me.

Stunned, I began feeling myself to make sure everything was intact. Nothing was broken, but my head throbbed from its contact with the seat back. I staggered to my feet and followed the others to the nearest exit. One by one, we stumbled off the ship and onto the surface of Fweam.

Once everyone was safely on the ground, the Queen went around to each of us to make sure no one was injured. Gurgatron and Tippers crawled under the ship to survey the damage while Bobby stood by and watched, a look of apprehension across his youthful face. After a few moments, the two pilots emerged.

"It doesn't look good, ma'am," Gurgatron told the Queen. "The quvvat assimilator is completely shot, and two of the oybmak gears were damaged in the crash."

"Can they be repaired?" the Queen asked calmly.

"They can, but it will take some time, and we don't have the parts in hand."

"The Layr is nearby," Quadrell pointed out. "Maybe the Twins can help us with supplies to repair the ship."

"We'll need more than supplies, I'm afraid," Gurgatron continued. "The magnetic activity in the Corridor is much stronger than I'd anticipated. We'll likely end up in the same boat the moment we take off."

"What do you suggest?" the Queen asked.

"An escort's what we need. The Fweamish Fleet is famous for its high-tech barrier shields that are impervious to magnetic rays. It is—unfortunately—a secretive proprietary technology that I've been trying to replicate for some time. Regardless, it's very effective. We'll need to request an escort to Hob to protect us from any further damage."

"That will likely be our best option," the Queen agreed. "Gurgatron, you and your crew stay with the ship and keep it safe from vandals. I will take Quadrell, Tippers, and the others to the Twins for help."

"Your Majesty, let us go on our own," Bobby interjected. "There's no need for you to trouble yourself."

"Our mission is very delicate," the Queen replied. "When the Twins know our purpose in traveling to Hob, they may be reluctant to help, out of fear for their own safety. It is only right that I secure their assistance in person."

"I understand," Bobby said in quiet acquiescence.

"I will need all of your help to maintain as low a profile as possible while I speak with the Twins," the Queen continued. "Our unannounced arrival on Fweam will likely turn some heads. The last thing we need is for news of our quest to precede us to Hob."

With that, Gurgatron and the six members of his crew were left behind to guard the ship, while the rest of us set off on foot toward the Layr. As we walked, I fell in step next to Quadrell and took the opportunity to ask him more about the recent change in our journey.

"So, who exactly are the Twins?" I began.

"Ninkus, Nipster, and Neti," Quadrell replied. "They govern Fweam together and are considered very knowledgeable."

"Wait, if there are three of them, why are they called the Twins?"

"Because no one has ever seen more than two of them at one time."

"How come?"

"You will see soon."

"But there are definitely three of them?"

"Most believe so. They comprise three distinct forms with three distinct voices. We just cannot see more than two of them at once. There are, of course, theories…" His voice trailed off.

"What else can you tell me about them?"

"Their parents were famous planet builders, but, sadly, the Twins were orphaned in the Great Planet Disaster of Yesteryear. We do not speak of it." This last part was said in a serious tone.

"I see," I responded. On that sober note, Quadrell and I continued the rest of the way in silence. It wasn't long before our destination was in sight.

The Layr was aptly named. Recessed into the side of a mountain, this cave-like structure was where the Twins spent most of their time. From this secure hideout of sorts, they governed the rest of Fweam.

When we arrived at the Layr's entrance, the Queen was instantly recognized, and our party was welcomed in without any fuss. Two alien assistants approached us once we were inside the complex. We stated our intention to meet with the Twins, and they relayed the message to their superiors. Presently, they returned with an update.

"The Twins will see you shortly in the Rose Room," the tall assistant announced.

"Also known as the Floribunda Rotunda," the short assistant pointed out eagerly.

The tall alien paused to glare at his companion, then turned to us and continued. "One thing you must know is that you are not to mention Death to them. As you are aware, the Twins' parents were killed in the Great Planet Disaster of Yesteryear. We do not speak of it." This last part was said in a hushed tone.

"We'll be sure not to bring it up," I promised.

"I had a cousin who choked to death on a fingernail," the short alien ventured. "He was a nail-biter, see, and—"

"That is hardly relevant," the tall alien interrupted severely. The short assistant hung his head.

Without further ado, the assistants ushered us into the rotunda. It was a magnificent room, although a conspicuous lack of roses belied its name. The domed ceiling was decorated to resemble the infinity of space. Intricate paintings of planets in gilded frames adorned the walls, and several planetary sculptures were perched upon pillars placed strategically throughout the floor. Encircling the room rose a high judicial-style bench, behind which three tall chairs framed three tall doorways in the wall, spaced evenly around the rotunda. Soft lighting illuminated the entire area.

We were led to the center of the room and told to stand and wait. At present, Ninkus, Nipster, and Neti each appeared in their respective doorways and seated themselves in their chairs around the bench. And it was in that moment that I understood why they were called the Twins.

Due to the even spacing of their chairs around the rotunda, the Twins maintained a distance of 120 degrees between each other at all times; thus, no matter how one turned, a person in the center of the room could keep, at most, two of them within eyes' view at once.

It was a curious setup, to be sure. But not as curious as the Twins themselves. Each looked identical to the others. They were hairless all over, with long, slender noses and chins. Their skin was smooth and mint green in hue, and their eyes were glassy—almost doll-like.

The tall assistant introduced our party, and the Twins rose momentarily from their seats in respect.

Ninkus spoke first. "We are truly honored by your presence, Your Majestiferousness."

"Please tell us the nature of your visit," Neti added.

The Queen wasted no time in apprising the Twins of our venture to reach Hob and save X@X from destruction. She detailed the abrupt and unfortunate interruption of our journey thus far and expressed the need for an escort by the Fweamish Fleet in order to continue safe and unhindered.

As the Queen spoke, the Twins sat back in their chairs, cocking their bald heads to the side and stroking their narrow chins. When the Queen finally finished with a plea for assistance, the Twins exchanged silent glances, as if pondering the full purport of the whole affair.

"This is quite a risky undertaking," Nipster said at last, addressing the Queen directly. "Have you considered the danger of It?"

"I am not here to be dissuaded from my quest, my good friends," the Queen said firmly, sidestepping his question with diplomatic ease. "I am here to ask for your help in fulfilling it."

"You can understand our reticence, I'm sure," Ninkus replied. "We do not wish to incur the ill favor of Asdf and Jkl."

"Indeed," Nipster chimed in. "The leaders of Hob do not like to be challenged. And while you may feel that you have nothing to lose by doing so, our fear is that Fweam may be included in the coming Purge as retribution for our interference. There is, of course, It to consider as well."

"Do not mistake us, Your Majescrumptiousness," Neti spoke up. "We respect your rule and will do as you command, but if you are leaving the choice to us, we must consider these things. Our parents built Fweam long ago, and we are bound by the Laws of Family and Fatherland to protect it."

"We are prepared to give you use of the planet Verv," Ninkus offered. "You and your people are welcome to relocate there should the Purge become a reality. It is a standard planet—unobtrusive and quiet—and will provide safety from Asdf and Jkl's whims."

"Yes, Verv should do nicely," agreed Nipster. Neti echoed this sentiment as well.

The Queen stood up straight, a flash of fire in her eyes. "As much as I appreciate your offer, my quest is not for a new planet. X@X is my home, and it shall remain such. What I am asking for is your assistance in protecting my home." The Queen moved to face each of them in turn as she continued. "I will not command your help, but I ask that you give it willingly. You will be greatly rewarded."

After a moment of silence, Neti broke it first. "Let us consult the Locust of Everseen. Perhaps his wisdom can help us make a decision."

"Yes, yes, bring in the Locust!" cried Nipster.

"Who is the Locust of Everseen?" I asked.

"He is a wise insect," replied Ninkus. "While your Wonder Wasps prophesy the future, the Locust of Everseen tells only of the past, and the deep secrets it holds that even men and aliens have forgotten."

A small silver cage was brought into the chamber by an assistant and placed before Ninkus. He opened the tiny door, and a grayish-green locust hopped out.

"Oh Wise One," began Ninkus, addressing the ancient insect, "the Queen of the Cosmos and her party are traveling to Hob to convince Asdf and Jkl to spare their planet from an upcoming Purge. Our assistance has been requested for this task. What say you?"

The locust's antennae twitched. "A story have I for Her Majesty," he called out in a feeble voice. "Listen, I pray you, to my words."

The Locust of Everseen began his tale.

"Long ago," he chirped, rubbing his legs together, "in the days of the Duprimsian Dynasty, the Men of the Great Forest desired more room to build their villages, so they approached Asdf and Jkl for permission to cut down the trees of the Forest. This request angered the rulers of Hob, for the Forest was, in their eyes, a beautiful and respected piece of artwork that decorated a portion of their sprawling playground. The men did not share this respect, however, and were very insistent that removing the trees was necessary to the survival of their civilization.

"After some deliberation, Asdf and Jkl granted their request but ordered that the men carry the felled trees upon their backs for the rest of their lives. Time went on, and the trees returned to their former glory, but the children of those men were born bent, as if the weight of those fallen trees still rested upon their shoulders. And so it is to this day: the Forest of the Hunched Men lives on as a cautionary tale to those who would challenge the Great Leaders of Hob."

With that, the locust hopped back in his cage. Ninkus shut the door, a look of triumph flashing across his face.

"The Locust of Everseen has spoken," he said. "It is as we suspected. This mission is not to end well. We cannot be of help, I'm afraid."

At this point, I had had enough. An insect's opinion had gotten me this far, and I was not about to let another's turn me back.

"What would your parents think?" I blurted out. A hush fell over the chamber. All eyes turned to look at me. Inside the silver cage, the locust cocked his head in curiosity. I knew I was breaking protocol by bringing up the Twins' parents, but I felt a heat rising in my chest that propelled the words from my mouth.

"They were planet builders, weren't they?" I continued. "They created planets, not destroyed them. Don't you think they would do anything in their power to save a planet from destruction if they were still alive?"

You could've heard a pin drop after my speech. All I could hear was the sound of my heart pounding as I waited for the worst to happen. I turned around and around, wondering which twin would speak first. Finally Nipster leaned forward.

"Who are you?" he asked flatly.

"I am the Earth-human that has been charged with convincing Asdf and Jkl to save X@X."

"Well, Earth-Human," he continued, "you have reminded us of our grief. That is very brazen of you."

He paused for a moment. My heartbeat quickened.

"But you are right," he said at last. "Our parents would have risked everything to save a planet from destruction."

I exhaled a sigh of relief. "So you'll help us, then?"

Neti spoke up. "Our parents *did* risk everything to save a planet from destruction. That is why they are dead. We are not our parents. We will not trade our own safety for the sake of another planet's."

Ninkus nodded in agreement. "We will give you the supplies you need to repair your ship, but we cannot give you the escort you request. Our assistants will aid you with the parts." With that, he and the others rose from their seats and turned to exit the rotunda.

Nipster was the last to speak. "We urge you to reconsider your mission, and fly home. Verv will be waiting for you if needed. The only thing waiting for you in Hob, I'm afraid, is It." Having given this final warning, he left the room through the doorway behind his chair.

With us alone, I turned to the others. "I-I'm so sorry," I stammered. "I guess my plan backfired."

"It is all right," the Queen assured me. "You were trying to help. The Twins are hard to convince. They had already set their minds against our mission. There is nothing that could have been said to persuade them."

Once we left the rotunda, the Twins' assistants led us to a storage unit deep within a dark tunnel of the Layr. It contained a vast array of mechanical gadgets and parts.

"Please take what you need," the tall assistant offered. Tippers and Quadrell took the lead, combing through the parts to find what was needed to repair the *Empress Galaqtica*. I hung back, mechanics not being my forte.

As I stood off to the side, watching the proceedings, I saw a movement out of the corner of my eye. It came from the shadows. I turned to face the murky darkness of the tunnel.

"Hello?" I called out. "Is anyone there?"

Chapter Aye

A figure slowly emerged from the shadows. It was a beautiful female alien with smooth orange skin and soft tendrils that snaked from her head. She wore a long white dress that danced delicately in the cool breeze from the tunnel.

"My name is Jemon-Aye," she said softly.

"Gemini?" I repeated.

"No, no…Jemon-Aye," she corrected me. "I shouldn't be talking to you, but I heard that you are trying to reach Hob. Is this true?"

I nodded, unsure whether I should trust this creature and say more.

"Well," she continued, "at the other end of Fweam—beyond the Dezert of Dan and the Not-So-Great Forest—is a science research center. Not many know this, but there is an old telepod there. You can use it to reach Hob."

My eyes widened at this valuable piece of information. "That's great!" I exclaimed. "Do you have Hob's telepod coordinates?" I remembered how Qarl's telepod had worked and knew that this was relevant info to have.

"Only one Man knows the coordinates that can teleport you to Hob. You will find him in the research center."

"Who is he?"

"I cannot tell you his name, nor even where in the facility he works. I cannot risk you writing it down and having the information fall into the wrong hands. All I can give you is this."

She handed me a folded note. I opened it cautiously. Inside were scrawled the words:

For Renn 6

Mark as Read

"What does it mean?" I asked. "Is Renn the guy we need to look for?"

"I'm afraid I cannot tell you more than what is written there," whispered Jemon-Aye. "But that clue contains all you need in order to know his whereabouts. When you find him, tell him I sent you."

"Why are you helping me?" I asked.

"Let's just say I'm repaying a debt," she replied with a smile. She turned to retreat into the dark tunnel but paused momentarily. "Oh, when you get to Hob, do be careful of It!"

"What is this 'It' everybody keeps talking about?" I asked, a little exasperated.

"Don't you know about the Portal?" Her voice trembled slightly.

"What portal?"

"The Portal Beyond Which No Man Awaits. You've never heard of It?"

"Not specifically. What is it?"

Jemon-Aye shivered. "It sits at the very Edge of the Universe. It is a place of eternal exile, built by Asdf and Jkl as a place of punishment."

"So Asdf and Jkl banish people through the portal?"

"Yes. And aliens."

"Why?"

Jemon-Aye shrugged and lowered her voice to a whisper. "Reasons Unknown. But what we do know is that those who are banished There never return, doomed to live a life of utter loneliness for the rest of their existence."

"How long has the portal been around?"

"Not terribly long. It has been around for a few mirqrulls now, but It is a fairly new device. And It has many of us gripped in fear. The thought of a life of loneliness is hard to face. Don't you know that being lonely is the worst thing in the Universe?"

I hadn't known. But I could tell she believed it, given the edge of terror to her voice.

"Please be careful," she pleaded before receding into the shadows.

"I will," I promised, watching as her white dress disappeared into the darkness.

After Jemon-Aye left, I stood lost in thought for a moment. *Why didn't the Queen tell me about the portal? Or Qarl, for that matter? Should I tell them about Jemon-Aye and the note? Should we risk the journey to the telepod, or try to repair the ship instead?* These questions bounced around in my head, their answers uncertain.

After spending some time deep in thought, I finally decided to confront the Queen. She was standing by the storage unit, supervising the search for replacement parts, but she turned to me as I approached her.

"I need to talk to you," I said.

"What is it?" she replied, giving me her full attention. We stepped away from the others to speak privately.

"Why didn't you tell me about The Portal Beyond Which No Man Awaits?" I asked bluntly.

The Queen paused for a moment, as if pondering how to reply. "I see you have found out about the portal."

"Yes, I have, and I want to know why you didn't tell me about it. Were you trying to hide it from me?"

"I think, in a way, I was," she admitted.

"Why?"

"I didn't want to worry you."

"With all due respect, don't you think it was only fair to tell me about this danger, especially before we started on our trip?"

"I am sorry. You are absolutely right. I was concerned that you would get caught up in the fear of the portal and decide not to come on this journey." The Queen took my hand in hers. "It was wrong of me not to be forthcoming with you."

"Is it a real danger, then?"

"It is a real portal, yes."

"And the banishment. It's real?"

"Real and permanent."

"What sort of crimes get someone sent there?"

"Reasons are never officially disclosed when an individual is banished. We find out that a disappearance has taken place but are not told specifically why."

"If that's true, why don't you try to stop Asdf and Jkl? This device has half your universe mad with fear. What if innocent beings are being banished?"

"I intend to do something, but my position is already precarious. I must act cautiously and deal with the Great Leaders in a way that does not further endanger the ones I protect and watch over. But if our mission to save X@X goes as planned, and we incur enough goodwill, perhaps I can convince them to close the portal as well."

It was worth a shot. Something wasn't making sense, however.

"I thought Asdf and Jkl were laid back," I said. "The more I hear about them, the more they sound quite tyrannical."

"They are very lazy when it comes to actively ruling the universe," the Queen replied. "They would much rather play and simply ignore the rest than be responsible rulers. But as you have seen yourself in how they play, they have a capricious nature, and this vagarious side can sometimes have a vindictive bent, particularly if they are challenged in any way."

"The portal sounds pretty serious though. Have they ever done anything this drastic or cold-blooded before?"

"No, this is as calculated as I've ever seen them get. As I've told you before, tensions have been escalating between us as of late. They clearly feel threatened by my rule. And just as I suspect of the upcoming purge, the establishment of the portal was almost certainly a desperate yet deliberate step to intimidate me and my followers—a step I refuse to let work as intended."

"You're not afraid. How come?"

"I want you to understand something about fear. Fear is a valid emotion that occupies a portion of our hearts and minds from time to time. However, if you let fear take over, it will set limits. Now, look at where we are! We live in space, a vast place *without* limits. Fear can have no rule here, else it will suffocate and destroy us.

"Besides," she continued, "not much is actually known about the portal, or what is on the other side. It is entirely possible that its terrors have been exaggerated, in which case our worry is needless."

"I see what you mean," I replied thoughtfully. The Queen seemed very wise, and I hoped she was right in her estimation of the portal.

I had one more question, however. "Is there anything else you're keeping from me?"

"Nothing." She met my gaze steadily, her eyes bright and honest. I chose to believe her.

"Now there's something I need to tell you," I said. "I met someone who may be able to help us."

Chapter J

The sun simmered on our backs as we trudged through the blinding sand. Ahead of me, Tippers and Bobby were locked in deep conversation. Beside me, Quadrell marched in silence. Behind me, Qarl was in consultation with the Queen, trying to convince her to change her title to Queen of the Qosmos. She—ever the diplomat—graciously declined his notion by saying that she did not wish to be haughty by adding another lofty *Q* to her title. He seemed to accept her explanation.

We were in the Dezert of Dan. I had finally told the Queen all about Jemon-Aye and the telepod on the other side of Fweam. After discussing our options with the others, the Queen had made the decision to send three of her soldiers back to Gurgatron and his crew with the parts to repair the ship, while the rest of us would journey to the science research center on foot and travel to Hob via the telepod. The plan was that, once the ship was in working order, Gurgatron would fly to the research facility and pick us up on our way back from Hob.

After leaving the Layr, we had been greeted with a vast expanse of desert. There was no way around the arid region, so we plodded through the dry sand, hoping that we would make it through without getting lost.

As we walked, I noticed many small pools scattered throughout the desert. These pools did not contain water, but a shiny gray putty substance.

"What is this stuff?" I asked Quadrell, who was still walking in silence beside me.

"It's magnemort," he replied dryly. "Magnetic death. It occurs naturally in the desert."

"Why is it called that? Is it dangerous?"

"It can be if you're wearing certain metals. During electrical storms, the putty becomes highly magnetized and attracted to specific metals. Because of this unique property, the substance is actually used in a form of execution on Fweam. The convicted is dressed in a special metal suit and placed in a pool of magnemort. The substance envelops the victim until they are suffocated."

"That sounds awful."

"It's reserved for a very specific set of crimes."

"I see." I was struck with how much Quadrell seemed to know about Fweam, from the Twins' parentage to the types of execution on this planet. "How do you know so much about this place?" I asked.

"My father is from Fweam," he replied.

"What about your mother?"

"She's from Madroniqa."

"Is it rare to have parents from two different planets?"

"It's becoming less unusual these days, but, as a child, I was the only one in my neighborhood who was bi-planetary. I was made fun of a lot."

"Why were you made fun of?"

"Others thought I was strange. As you can see, I have the eyes of my father in the front of my head and the eyes of my mother in the back. They change color based on my mood. I cannot hide who I am or what I am feeling. The others thought an alien with two sets of color-changing, mood-betraying eyes was weird." As if on cue, Quadrell's eyes turned a deep brown while he recalled his difficult past.

"How did you overcome all that?"

"My parents were very supportive and taught me to never let others get in the way of my success. With their encouragement, I was able to block out the ignorance of those around me and keep striving for my dreams. That's not to say it was easy, but I did my best."

"What happened next?"

"I joined the Space Pilot Academy and began training. Sadly, I discovered that the prejudiced attitudes that had marred my childhood persisted into adulthood. Many of my peers and professors believed it was unnatural for aliens from two different planets to mix. I found many barriers that I struggled to overcome placed in front of me, obstacles that others did not seem to encounter. I was passed over for many training missions, and, as a result, my education progressed much more slowly than usual."

"That's terrible!" I shook my head. "What ended up happening?"

"When Gurgatron assumed the role of Academy Director, he took notice of me and brought me under his wing. He fired the discriminating instructors and got me a job in the Queen's employ. I'm still in training, but I hope to become a pilot soon."

"If only the haters could see you now, right?"

"If they could, I'd want them to understand that prejudice and ignorance do not stay isolated. They are dangerous things that spread perniciously and have real-life effects on their targets."

"That is so true," I agreed.

"Hey, look at those two," Quadrell said abruptly, nudging me with his elbow and nodding toward Bobby and Tippers. They were walking in step, deep in conversation, their shoulders occasionally brushing together. "What do you think?" Quadrell asked.

"I think they like each other," I replied.

"So do I," he concurred. He maintained a serious expression on his face, but his eyes turned green with mischievous delight. I guessed that he would never admit it, but I knew he was being filled with an urge to embarrass the pair, an impulse that is quite natural to feel when one witnesses blossoming love in others.

After a time, the Queen and I swapped places, she joining Quadrell to discuss particulars of the journey ahead and I falling in line with Qarl at the rear of the group. The two of us journeyed in silence for a while.

As we continued on our way, the wind began to pick up speed, catching the grains of sand and flinging them into our faces. The Queen wrapped her cape around her face to shield against the onslaught; the rest of us used our shirts. We bent our heads down into the wind and pressed onward, hoping that the storm would pass quickly, but it only grew stronger.

Crackling bolts of lightning began to strike the ground all around us, and the pools of magnemort gurgled in response. Visibility grew steadily worse until I could barely see the others around me.

Before Qarl faded into the dust, I grabbed his hand and planted myself into the ground. I dared not move another step lest I become hopelessly lost.

"I'm stopping here!" I shouted, hoping the others would hear me and halt as well, but the howling wind captured my words and threw them back at me. I was becoming disoriented. Everywhere I turned, the same swirling brown view met my eyes.

My shirt was little protection from the fine grains of sand that danced all around me. The grit was getting into my mouth, stinging my eyes, burning my nose—I couldn't breathe. I collapsed to the ground, my hand still gripping Qarl's.

Everything went dark.

π π π π π

I woke up in a sweat, the hot sun beating down on my face. The sky was a bright blue, and the air was still and clear. Rising to my knees, I looked over to see Qarl lying a few feet away, stirring as well. He moaned as the blinding sun struck his upturned face.

Stumbling to my feet, I looked around. None of the others were in sight. Flat sand stretched as far as the eye could see in every direction. I walked over and nudged Qarl.

"Are you ok?"

"I think so," he croaked miserably. "Where are the others?"

"I don't see them," I replied, gazing toward the horizon in every direction, hoping to catch a flash of iridescent purple from the Queen's cape.

Stepping forward into the dry sand, I cupped my hands around my mouth and shouted. My voice carried across the flat land, but none returned to greet my ears. Qarl and I were alone.

"Get up, Qarl," I instructed. "We have to keep moving." I struggled to swallow, my throat parched. I was so thirsty. I couldn't remember ever being this thirsty. We needed to find water—fast.

Qarl staggered to his feet. "Which direction do we go?" he asked.

It was a good question. I had no idea. Bobby had the only compass. My eyes strained as I scanned the horizon, looking for a recognizable landmark, but everything looked the same.

And then I remembered something.

"Our shadows! I vaguely remember our shadows being in front of us as we were walking. Qarl, do you know if Fweam's rotation is faster or slower than Earth's?"

Qarl scratched his horn in thought. "I think it's slower."

"Then the sun that cast our shadows before the sandstorm should be in nearly the same spot now, which means we just need to align ourselves so that our shadows face forward again."

"Are you sure?" Qarl asked doubtfully.

"Not entirely, but it's the best I have to go on."

"Doesn't the saying go 'Don't run from your shadow, but don't follow it either'?" He grinned weakly, still maintaining a sense of humor despite the dire situation.

"You're not being very helpful, Qarl," I replied, not amused.

"Sorry."

After determining our direction of travel based on our shadows, Qarl and I began walking. I hoped that we were heading in the right direction. The hot sun continued to beat down on us and showed no signs of abating. Qarl and I had no water to quench our growing dehydration, and I knew that it was critical that we make it out of the desert as soon as possible.

To pass the time and ward off boredom, Qarl and I chatted about various things as we walked. We started by discussing Quadrell.

"He's quite an interesting alien," I noted.

"I know," Qarl agreed. "I miss him already." He sighed, downcast.

I rolled my eyes. "The poor guy's probably glad to have a break from you following him around."

"Can I help it if he's more interesting than you?" Qarl retorted.

"Ouch."

"Besides, he's the only one that seems to sympathize with me on the tragic loss of my precious teletransportube. He cheered me up by telling me about a brand-new model the Academy is helping design: the Kevin.11!" Qarl's face became animated as he described the new machine. "I can't wait to get my hands on it. I've been bugging the Queen about it all day."

"And?"

"Her Majestiliciousness is undecided."

Qarl's use of this singular appellation then prompted a conversation segue into why he and other aliens had a penchant for using elaborate titles (always capitalized, of course). He explained that it was due to an innate sense of fear that most aliens possessed, which often manifested itself as respectful deference for those in higher positions or reverential awe for important and mighty things. Incessant capitalization was a side effect of these feelings; not limited to titles, the uppercase treatment was extended to many an object, species, and even phrase—anything that elicited such deep-seated emotions.

I then asked Qarl how he and other aliens could tell when someone was not spelling, hyphenating, or capitalizing a word correctly when they said it. He shrugged and told me that he couldn't explain why most aliens had this gift of ultrasensitive hearing, just as I couldn't explain why humans had the garrulous gift of gab.

I also touched on Qarl's unique and obsessive love of the letter *Q*, but he responded by bringing up my addictive love of candy. With neither of us willing to spend time defending his fixation to the other, we ended up transitioning into conversing about my newfound discovery of the portal's existence.

Suddenly, I heard rustling in the sand behind me. Turning, I saw a lone ostrich strutting along in our footsteps. We slowed and moved to the side so that he could pass us, but he adjusted his gait to match ours, remaining behind us at all times.

"Can I help you?" I asked at last, stopping and turning to face the giant bird.

The ostrich shuffled over to me on his gangly legs. "I'm quite certain you *could,* and perhaps even *would,* were I in need of assistance. As it stands, however, I am not in such need."

"Um, ok then. Why are you following us?"

"Oh, I'm not following you. We just happen to be going to the same place at the same time."

"How do you know where I'm going?"

"Because it is the same place I am going."

"And where is that?"

"Not Here."

There was a brief silence.

"Would you be more specific?" I pressed further.

"If I were more specific, then I would be less fuzzy." He blinked. I blinked. He cocked his bristled head and ruffled his black feathers at me.

"Was that supposed to be a joke?" I asked.

"Am I supposed to suppose that you are supposing I supposed it to be so?"

"Fuck, you're worse than Qarl."

"Hey!" Qarl objected.

"Your friend is offended," the ostrich pointed out.

I shrugged indifferently. "Eh, he'll be fine." Qarl glared at me, but I ignored him. "Look," I continued, "it was nice meeting you, but we gotta run."

"I can run," the bird replied. "My top speed is 0.00377193 miles per mirkron. What's yours?"

"Um, I don't really know."

"Shall we race and find out?"

"No, I can't. I'm sorry."

"You can't? Your legs look fine to me." He bent his long pink neck down and pecked rudely at my legs with his sharp bill.

"Ow! Stop it!" I yelled. Qarl snorted with laughter.

"Your friend is amused by our conduct," the ostrich noted. "Shall I continue?" He leaned down toward my legs again.

"No!" I said firmly, backing away. "Look, just leave us alone."

"But if you two are together, how can you be alone?"

I sighed with exasperation. "The Locust of Everseen was right," I muttered to myself. "This journey is a nightmare."

"Locust? What locust?" the ostrich asked eagerly, turning his head wildly in every direction. "I love locusts ever so much. They are quite tasty and very filling." He smacked his bill hungrily.

I sensed an opportunity and wasn't about to let it pass by. "Well, there's a big juicy locust back at the Layr just waiting to be invited for dinner."

"Ooo, which way? Which way?" The ostrich began to dance excitedly, flapping his flightless wings with delighted anticipation. I pointed behind us, and before I could say another word, the ostrich took off running as fast as his long legs would carry him.

"What a weird fucking bird," I commented, watching him recede rapidly into the distance.

"Fuqqing," Qarl corrected automatically. I shot him a glare.

"C'mon, let's keep going. We've wasted too much time already."

With the ostrich gone at last, Qarl and I continued through the desert, becoming more and more faint as we walked. The miles seemed endless, and still nothing appeared on the horizon.

"I have a question for you," Qarl said slowly, breaking the silence. His voice sounded odd.

"What is it?"

"Do alcoholic camels, like, drink once and they're buzzed all year?" he slurred. Qarl was clearly becoming delirious, and I was not far behind.

"Qarl, let's keep walking," I replied, disregarding his bizarre question. "We need to make it out of this desert as soon as possible."

There was a pause, then he spoke again.

"A sinus infection is all in your head."

I smirked but kept walking, trying to ignore him. He wasn't finished, however.

"The best things in life are free, right?"

I sighed. "That's what they say."

"And there's no such thing as a free lunch, right?"

"That's also something they say."

"Ergo, lunch is not one of the best things in life. Am I right?"

I sighed again. "Shut up, Qarl."

"Wait, wait, I have another one. What do you get when you rub salt in a wound?"

"I don't know, Qarl. What do you get?" I resigned myself to the lame punchline that would inevitably follow.

"A really tasty wound!" He chortled loudly as he said this.

I couldn't help but crack a smile. "You're disgusting, dude. Now, keep walking."

We continued plodding through the dusty sand. Every so often, we would spy what appeared to be a pool of water. Qarl would leap forward with a cry and run to the spot, only to be greeted by the sight of more sand. The cruel work of mirages was out in full force, and, with every disappointment, we were becoming more and more desperate.

After the umpteenth deception was played on us by the wicked desert, Qarl fell to his knees with a wail, clutching fistfuls of sand and flinging them in every direction. I didn't have the energy to corral him any longer. I was so thirsty. My dry lips were cracking, and my mouth didn't have enough saliva to moisten them. My tongue began to stick to the roof of my mouth.

I knelt beside Qarl, who was sobbing quietly, his body so dehydrated that no tears fell from his eyes. I wondered if this would be the place where we breathed our last.

My thoughts turned to my mother. I wondered what she was doing now, and if she missed me at all. Would I ever see her again?

I looked once more at the horizon through blurred vision. A dark mass hovered in the distance. I rubbed my eyes, blinked, and looked again.

The shape was a group of palm trees.

"Qarl, look!" I cried excitedly, nudging my companion, who was curled up in the fetal position.

"What is it?" he slurred.

"It's an oasis! Come on!"

"It's just another mirage. You'll see. Just let me die." Qarl rolled over, turning his face upward toward the blazing sun, as if accepting his fate.

"It's not a mirage," I protested. "It's a group of palm trees. And where there are trees in the desert, there's water!"

I yanked on Qarl's arm until he stumbled to his feet. Half pulling, half dragging him through the sand, I made my way toward the oasis, as though it were a safe harbor and I a floundering ship. As we neared the trees, I could spot a pool of the clearest water I had ever seen.

It was real.

Reaching the oasis at last, I collapsed at the water's edge and lapped up the lifesaving liquid like a thirsty dog. Qarl did the same. The cool water kissed my lips and ran down my throat in refreshing rivers, banishing my thirst and bringing life back into my weary body. After drinking my fill, I leaned back in the shade of a palm tree with a satisfied sigh, feeling drained yet relieved.

"You ok, Qarl?" I asked.

"Yeah, I'm good," he responded between gulps, still attacking the water feverishly. At length, he leaned back and wiped the droplets of water from his mouth. Reclining against a tree across from me, he closed his eyes and folded his small hands across his stomach.

We both lay in silence for a while, our bodies exhausted. Only the tinkling music of the rippling pool and the gentle rustling of palm fronds met our ears.

"Qarl?" I asked at last.

"Yeah?" He opened one eye.

"Tell me more about the portal," I ventured, struck with a sudden curiosity to know more.

Qarl leaned forward. "What do you want to know?"

"How does it work? I mean, if the whole point is to be alone for the rest of your existence, what happens once two or more people are banished?"

"It's a multidimensional portal. Each Person that is banished there occupies a separate dimension. They can all see the same space but cannot see, hear, or interact with each other."

"That sounds…lonely."

"Well, that's the point." He picked at the grass around the pool.

"It sure has a lot of aliens freaked out. It took me forever to find out about the portal because so many of them won't even call it by name."

Qarl rolled his eyes. "I wouldn't let their fear be contagious. The portal isn't as bad as many think it is."

"How do you know?"

Qarl shifted a bit. "Oh, you know how aliens are. Always extra fearful and whatnot."

"You're an alien, and you don't seem bothered by it."

Qarl chuckled dryly. "Guess I'm weird, then. Say, we should get going," he said, abruptly changing the subject.

"Are you sure?" I asked, concerned. "Don't you want to rest for a bit more?"

"Nope, I'm good. I just want to get out of this fuqqing desert."

With that, we set off on our way, renewed energy in our veins. After several more miles, we could finally see the edge of the desert ahead, a little village beckoning us from the outskirts. We raced toward it eagerly, ready to leave the unforgiving desert behind for good.

We were still quite thirsty from our time in the desert, so we stopped by the only pub in town: The Forbidden Letter. We discovered the eccentric owner loved every letter except one, so no one frequenting his pub could use the forbidden letter in speech, text, or even thought while on the premises.

The bouncer provided us with envelopes, telling us he could not utter the letter himself, but it would be written inside for our reference. Ripping mine open timidly, I wondered which letter would be prohibited. I hoped it would be uncommon, like Z or *J*.

I stood still, looking curiously through the contents of the envelope. One folded file occupied the interior. Slowly I withdrew the sheet, unfolding it gently. I could not believe my eyes.

Only two tiny scribbles, written tidily in brown ink, sullied the bright-white scroll I held in my trembling fingers. Together they represented both versions of the impermissible letter. The towering first form consisted of two tilting poles—one inclining left, the other to the right, their top ends joined together—with one single crosspiece supporting the middle. The shorter second form utilized less ink, to be sure, but nonetheless shone proudly from the document, its roundness merging tightly with one extremity drifting to the right.

"*This* is the forbidden letter?" I questioned, stunned. "This one must never be used? But how could we not? It's just so common!"

"We could order beer or wine," my friend suggested helpfully, looking over my shoulder. His envelope held corresponding contents to mine.

"But it won't even be possible for me to refer to you by—you know, your proper moniker," I replied. "I'm getting quite dizzy just thinking how I'm going to circumvent using this vowel!"

"Well, if not being permitted to use this letter is going to be too difficult for us, then let's go," he responded.

So we left to visit the next town.

π π π π π

Qarl and I stopped on the dusty road at the edge of the next village. Before us loomed a large wooden sign. Brightly painted letters welcomed us to Nonsense Town.

"What a weird name for a town," I remarked to Qarl.

He nodded in agreement. "It really is."

As we were soon to find out, the place was much weirder than its name.

[Editor's note: Once again, we must beg your leave to continue the next portion of the narrative in poetry, as the author felt this was the best way to proceed.]

Time runs back, amoebas quack,
And sausage rolls fly upside down,
While Pluto pats fat alley cats
All day and night in Nonsense Town.

It's often seen that corn is green,
And seaweed floats in barber chairs.
And piglets sound within the ground
As if the mayor lost his hair.

Pulpits race, and sand gives chase
When bottles rob the local store.
And steeples roll through dirty holes
While burning matches as a chore.

Stoves are cold and made of gold
And talk through eyes of shining brass.
Old pancakes pop, and bubbles flop
Because they shatter too much glass.

Chameleons fly without the sky,
Atop their butter and their bread,
While toilets gape through masking tape
At placemats jumping off their beds.

Bikers quit when they get bit
By angry mobs of muenster cheese.
And great white sharks spit tally marks
Through fields of scrumptious golden peas.

Now if you think that snow is pink
And some is nothing all at once,

You may try to catch your eye,
And maybe not be called a dunce.

So take your pick and choose your stick
And travel highways up and down,
But if you find you've lost your mind,
You might try living in this town!

Needless to say, Qarl and I left just as quickly as we had come.

Chapter K

The next town we encountered was Maryville. I suggested that Qarl and I split up for a bit to try to find the others more quickly. Qarl agreed and ducked down a side street while I continued up the main thoroughfare into the center of town.

Something seemed…"off"…about Maryville. Despite the presence of inhabitants, it was quiet—too quiet. I continued up the street, hoping to catch a glimpse of our party, but saw no one I recognized.

Maryville was a somber place. Everywhere I looked, aliens wandered in a trancelike state, their heads down and their faces crestfallen. Occasionally a sob would break through the veil of somberness and echo hauntingly off the building facades. I cautiously approached one of these sad creatures and asked what the matter was.

"I mourn," the alien replied in a pitiful voice.

"I can see that," I responded gently. "But what is wrong?"

The creature looked up at me with watery eyes. "I mourn the Absence of Mary," he whispered.

"Who is Mary?" I queried further. The alien stared at me for a long moment before replying.

"I don't know."

With that, the alien turned and slinked away into the shadows, leaving me feeling more than a bit confused and uneasy.

Desperate to find out what was going on, I approached another alien, only to receive the exact same response. Again and again I tried to obtain an answer from each creature I encountered, but to no avail. I finally gave up and plopped down on the steps of the nearest building.

"Do you want to know what is going on, stranger?" a quiet voice asked from behind me.

I turned and looked up. I had chosen the steps of a temple to rest upon, and from its shadows emerged a dark figure. He was dressed in a simple robe with mysterious symbols embroidered into it. From his neck hung a silver chain, a tiny sphere of clouded glass attached in the front.

I stood up as he approached me. "I don't mean to intrude," I told him, "but I am very concerned by what I see. Can you tell me what is happening here? Why all the sorrow?"

"We mourn," the dark figure replied. "We all mourn."

I rolled my eyes slightly at this revelation. "Yes, that is abundantly clear," I retorted. Before I could continue, the alien resumed his explanation.

"We mourn the Absence of Mary."

"WHO is Mary?" I asked, thoroughly exasperated. The alien paused for a moment. "Let me guess," I continued. "You don't know. Nobody seems to know." I threw up my hands in frustration.

"Nobody seems to know," the dark figure repeated robotically.

"But you still mourn her anyway."

The alien nodded. "Indeed, we still mourn her."

"Why would you mourn someone or something you don't even know?"

"We grieve her Absence, for that is a sorrowful thing. It is our way." A single tear slid down the alien's cheek as he said this.

"Well, why did she leave?" I asked, anticipating the answer in my head.

"Nobody seems to know," the alien whispered cryptically. "But perhaps if we mourn her Absence enough, she will return to us."

"And do what?" I pressed. "Rule the land? Teach the nation? Save you from yourselves?"

The alien smiled at me slightly before silently gliding backward into the shadows of the temple interior.

"Well?" I called out after him. "What's going to happen if she returns?"

A thin, whispery echo wafted from the darkness: "Nobody seems to knooooow..."

Beyond frustrated, I leapt from my seat on the temple steps and ran into the street, looking for Qarl. I found him down a side alley, standing on a soapbox and surrounded by a crowd of aliens. As I approached, I could hear his pinched, nasally voice speaking.

"My fellows," he was saying, "since our great Mary left us, her Absence has been felt greatly by all. Shall we not then mourn until her return? Shall we not drown our sorrows with more sorrow? Shall we not grieve the greatest grief that could ever be grieven?"

I couldn't believe my ears. *What happened to Qarl?* I moved forward to the edge of the crowd, which was hanging eagerly on Qarl's every word. He was not finished.

"Cry out, my friends!" he instructed. "Let sobs break forth from your air passages, and let us all wail in synchronicity. Mary is Absent, and we must drink the sorrow this brings us."

He lifted a silver flask to his thick purple lips as he said this and took a gulp of liquid. In response, the crowd erupted into doleful screeches of woe, their voices converging into a cacophonic chorus that viciously assaulted the eardrums.

Clapping my hands over my ears to block out the horrid sound, I moved farther into the crowd and strained to get Qarl's attention. He caught my eye momentarily, and I motioned frantically for him to come with me. Nodding slightly, he stepped somberly from his soapbox and cleared his throat loudly, his phlegmatic utterance breaking through the crowd's vociferous lamentations. All fell silent and turned to give him attention.

"My planetary brethren," he said gravely, "I must take leave of you briefly. Please continue mourning in my absence."

At the mention of the word "absence," his voice faltered, and tears welled up in his eyes. A thoughtful alien standing nearby placed a reassuring tentacle on his arm.

"I hope to return very soon to you all," he continued. "Grievings and lamentations!"

"Grievings and lamentations," the crowd murmured back, parting to let him through. Once Qarl was free of the throng, I grabbed his arm and pulled him to the side of the alleyway.

"Qarl, *what the hell* are you doing?" I asked him, confusion and concern in my voice.

Qarl looked up at me, his eyes glazed over and his lips trembling. "I am mourning the Absence of Mary."

"But why? Are you ok? What have they done to you?" I peppered Qarl with questions, but he seemed unfazed by my interrogation.

"She is…Absent," he replied with a hiccup. Something was off about Qarl (and that was saying a lot). He seemed…

"Are you…drunk?" I asked incredulously. I snatched the silver flask from his hand and held it to my nose. Yep, Qarl was definitely drunk.

I turned back to the crowd, most of whom were still weeping at various decibel levels.

"Who gave this to him?" I shouted above the din. No one paid me any mind. "HEY!" I yelled louder. "Shut the hell up!"

An instant hush fell over the crowd as all eyes turned to me. Qarl stumbled drunkenly beside me and reached for the flask, which I kept out of reach, despite his slurred protests. I was angry now, and I was about to let the crowd have it.

"What is wrong with all of you? Huh? Why are you standing around, wailing, getting my friend drunk in the middle of the day? Why are you mourning someone you don't even know, someone you've never met, someone who should have no impact on your lives?"

The crowd remained silent, staring at me with unblinking eyes.

"Why can't you do something productive with your time instead of spending it grieving over some mysterious person who isn't even here?"

I had my mouth open to continue when a disturbance at the edge of the crowd caught my eye. Two soldiers dressed in full regalia were parting the crowd and coming my way.

"You!" one shouted at me. "Come with us at once!"

"What for?" I countered. "I'm not doing anything wrong."

"He is besmirching our beloved Mary's memory," an alien spoke up unhelpfully.

"What memory!?!" I yelled. "You all have no memory of this woman." The soldiers had reached me by this point and grasped my arms to pull me away. I started to resist but thought better of it when I saw the large swords they carried on their hips.

"You have committed a grave sin," one of them told me roughly. "You and your blue friend must go before the council." With that, they pulled us away from the crowd.

Qarl and I were brought into the center of the village, where an ugly gray building stood. This was the council hall, we were told, where we would answer for our crimes. Once inside, we were each locked in a holding cell to wait until the council was ready to hear our case.

A few hours later, we were both summoned to the courtroom. It was a vast room, blandly decorated and somber in appearance. Guards were posted at every exit, while the crowd from earlier filled seats in a spectators' section. All eyes turned to Qarl and me as we were led into the courtroom by the two soldiers who had arrested us. Incoherent whispers met my ears as the crowd murmured amongst themselves.

A wood-paneled judge's bench occupied the far end of the space. Behind it sat twelve council members and a judge. Positioned in the center behind them was a large sphere made of clouded glass. I recognized it as a much larger version of the one the temple alien had worn round his neck. I wondered what the gigantic glass ball represented.

My attention turned to the judge. She had piercing eyes and a face frozen into a mournful scowl. Gray hair was piled atop her head, complementing her gray-tinged skin. On each hand she had ten bony fingers, which she tapped annoyingly on the bench.

The most intriguing thing about her appearance, however, was a small gray rain cloud that hovered above her head, following her around whenever she moved. Occasionally a drop would fall and land on her face, cascading down her cheek like a tear.

Qarl and I were ordered to stand before the bench. We complied, and the soldiers stepped aside. The judge raised her hand, and the room fell silent.

"It has been reported that you have been challenging our way of life to the village folk," she said to me, reading off a large scroll.

"I've been questioning why everyone is mourning some woman they don't even know," I clarified.

"That is not your place!" she barked, her mournful expression turning swiftly into one of anger. "This is our way of life, and you must respect that."

"But who is Mary?" I asked, still insistent on proving the ridiculousness of this whole venture.

"That is an irrelevant question. We need only to mourn her Absence."

"Even *you* don't know anything about this Mary!" I exclaimed, completely exasperated that no one but me seemed to recognize how bizarre this situation was.

"We know enough," she retorted. "We know our Mary is great, that she is Absent, and that we must mourn this Absence until she return to us in the year Two Thousand When, as saith the prophecy:

'In the year Two Thousand When,
Mary shall return again.'"

"And so may it be," murmured the crowd in unison.

"And so may it be," she repeated. "This is all we need to know."

"That is utterly stupid," I blurted out with a sarcastic chuckle. "Your whole lives revolve around this mystery woman that no one seems to know anything about. What's the point of all this?"

As I said this last statement, a crack suddenly appeared in the glass sphere behind the bench, with a noise like ice breaking. The crowd gasped, and the judge leapt to her feet.

"Stop!" she ordered. "You are harming the bubble with your questions."

"What are you talking about?"

She gestured toward the glass spheroid. "This bubble protects our way of life and must not be harmed."

"Well, I think your way of life is ridiculous." The crack in the glass widened with a groan as I said this. The crowd collectively inhaled at a higher pitch.

"Silence!" cried the judge. The cloud above her head darkened. "Speak no further, or your punishment will be most severe."

"What, are you going to mourn me to death?" I joked. The crack split into three branches, and a few aliens fainted.

"ENOUGH!" shrieked the judge. Her eyes flashed, and thunder rumbled from her cloud. "The council must now decide your fate."

The deliberation was brief, likely due to both my obvious culpability in "harming the bubble" and a frantic desire on their part to prevent further damage. After a short time, the judge banged her gavel, cleared her throat, and spoke.

"The council has reached a verdict!"

The crowd leaned in, hanging on her every word.

"We shall keep your friend Qarl with us, as there is still a chance for his indoctrination," the judge said to me decisively. "You, however…" (here she paused for effect) "…must be shunned!"

The crowd began to chant rhythmically, "Shun! Shun! Shun! Shun! Shun!" She hushed them and continued.

"Let the shunning begin!"

With that, she and the council swiveled their chairs away from me while the entire crowd turned their backs. Qarl drunkenly complied as well, turning his blue head away.

Silence reigned in the chamber for a few moments. At length, one member of the council tentatively turned my way to see my reaction, which remained unchanged. He cleared his throat.

"Erm, Your Honor, the shunning appears not to be working as intended."

The judge gave an exasperated sigh and turned back around to face me. The crowd followed suit.

"Very well," she said sternly. "Given your grievous crimes, we have no choice but to turn you over to..." (here she paused again for effect) "...the Vream!"

The crowd collectively gasped at the news.

"The who?" I asked.

"The Vream of Fweam!" she responded dramatically. She rose from the bench, walked over to me, and thrust a black flask into my hand.

"Drink!" she ordered.

"What is it?" I asked.

"It is the Elixir of the Damned," she replied coldly with an unnecessary flourish of her hand. The crowd *ooooh*ed softly behind her.

"Oh...ok then." I lifted the flask to my lips and took a tentative sip. The Elixir of the Damned was clearly ginger ale.

"This is clearly ginger ale," I pointed out. She raised her hand as if to strike me.

"Shut up!" she ordered. "You must drink it."

How disappointing, I thought, staring at the flask of tepid liquid. *At least Qarl got to drink regular ale.*

"Drink it all!" she hurried me. "Every drop must be taken for the Vream. The Elixir marks you as his."

Fuck it, I told myself, and, tilting my head back, I drained the flask. No sooner had the flask left my lips than it was snatched out of my hands and given to a guard. Raising her arm, the judge pointed to the door.

"Let us go offer him to the Vream!"

I was led downstairs, out the door, and to the edge of town. Council and crowd followed us. Night had fallen, and a black night it was. Nary a star twinkled in the sky, as if each was hiding its face from my impending doom.

We finally stopped at the edge of a thick wood. The judge faced the dark trees with a sober expression on her severe features.

"O Vream!" she called out into the void. "O Vream of Fweam! Take your child of darkness. He waits here for you."

Nothing happened.

"O Vream!" she repeated. "O Vream of Fweam! Take your child of darkness. Take him now!"

A pair of red eyes shone suddenly from the shadows. The judge stepped back in response, and I involuntarily followed suit.

"'Tis the Vream!" she whispered breathlessly.

"'Tis! 'Tis! 'Tis! 'Tis!" the crowd repeated in a louder whisper. She turned and hushed them.

Placing her bony hand firmly on my back, she instructed, "Go and meet your new master."

I hesitated, as the average sane person would have. I knew that glowing red eyes were pretty much the universal sign of anger, malice, and/or all things evil.

"You know, I'm not exactly in the market for a new master," I started to say, but the judge's hand pressed harder into my back, sending pain shooting through my shoulders. Wriggling away from her forceful push, I stepped gingerly toward the darkness…and toward those foreboding eyes.

The eyes seemed to glow redder as I approached, but I'm sure my gripping fear had nothing to do with it. As I continued into the shadows, I could hear Qarl drunkenly singing in the crowd behind me.

"You got in trouble for harming the bubble," he slurred. I really wanted to smack his head off again. Much to my annoyance, the crowd eagerly took up the chant as I stepped farther into the darkness.

I had almost reached the eyes when I stopped suddenly. The eyes were rising. Up, up they traveled, until they were floating a good ten feet above my head. It was then that I noticed that the eyes were attached to a body, and that the body belonged to a giant shadowy beast, and that the beast was standing up.

I felt a wave of heat wash over me as the beast rose up on its hind legs. And then, in the next instant, a hot yellow light enveloped my body. I dropped to the ground in a panic. Looking up, I saw a massive flame raging over my head. And in that moment, I knew.

The beast was a dragon. *Yay.*

As I continued staring up at the fire-breathing monster, the flame died away. Ever so menacingly, the creature turned its gaze downward to me.

I gulped in terror. *Do something,* I told myself. *Don't just let him fry you!* In that moment, I knew what I had to do.

I crouched down and began to execute a perfect barrel roll toward the bushes. Alas, it was not to be. No sooner had I begun my roll than I felt my body leaving the ground.

Twisting my head around, I looked with terror into the glowing eyes of the fearsome beast barely an inch away from my face. The dragon had picked me up with his dreadful claw and was carrying me away into the trees. The clamoring voices of the crowd grew quieter in the distance.

I was truly fucked.

Chapter L

"Decimus Minimus the Sixteenth!" a voice thundered from the darkness. "Put the young man down at once!"

The creature complied instantly, dumping me unceremoniously to the dirt before skulking away into the shadows. I scrambled to my feet and turned to face the commanding voice.

Before me stood an old man, bent and withered but with a kind face. He wore a long scratchy robe and leather sandals, and a flowing white beard touched his waist.

Finding my breath after being flung to the ground, I ventured hesitantly, "Are—are you the Vream?"

The old man chuckled dryly and shrugged his shoulders. "I suppose," he answered. "Do they still call me that?" I nodded wordlessly.

He continued, "I have so many names that I sometimes forget my own. Those on the other side of Fweam call me the Wiser Miser, these ones call me the Vream…it's hard to keep track."

"What are you going to do to me?" I asked cautiously.

"Absolutely nothing," the old man replied. "I don't know why they keep sending outsiders over here. When Decimus grew to his size, they must have assumed we wanted sacrifices. They're an odd bunch, they are." I wasn't about to disagree with that statement.

"So I'm free to go?" I asked.

"You are…although I'll offer you what I offer all the others who drop my way: a tour of my home, a few pearls of wisdom, and a well-wish as you go on your way. But you are under no obligation to accept any of those."

I hesitated. I really needed to get going and find a way to rescue Qarl before things got worse for him, but it was already dark, and I was honestly in no mood to rush back to my former captors.

"Ok," I decided. "I'll stay for a bit."

The old man nodded and led me down a short path to a small hut. The place was made of dirt and sticks and looked to have been built by the hands of the old man himself. The doorway was covered with an intricately woven blanket, which the man parted, motioning me to step through.

The inside of the humble abode was bare, save for the most essential items: a bed with one blanket, a table with a lone plate and cup on it, and a single chair. One object in particular, however, caught my eye. In the very center of the dwelling, positioned on an ancient tree stump, was a large fish tank.

I stepped forward to get a closer look. The glass was pristine, the water clear, and dozens of brightly colored fish swam in circles inside the gigantic enclosure.

"I like your fish tank," I remarked as the old man entered his home behind me.

"Are they in a fish tank?" he responded. "Or are we in their human tank?"

I paused, a bit taken aback by the idea. My mind flew to considering the ramifications of such a peculiar concept. Before my lips could form a reply, however, the old man motioned for me to take a seat in the chair while he took his repose on the edge of the bed. I seated myself and was about to ask him more about the fish tank when he spoke first.

"Please tell me about your adventure, and how you ended up on the bad side of the council of Maryville."

I recounted the whole story from the beginning, starting with my summoning from Earth and concluding with the unfortunate ending of my encounter with the Maryvillians. As I spoke, I knew that I shouldn't have been telling this man about the Queen's top secret mission, but an instinctive trust overcame my inhibitions, and I found myself telling him everything about our quest to reach Hob and save X@X.

The old man shook his head as I finished. "The Maryvillian council is truly dangerous. More and more outsiders have been sent my way lately. Some for questioning their way of life, as you did…others for various sins."

"What sorts of sins get you sent here?"

"I honestly can't even remember. I've been exposed to so many belief systems in my life that it is hard to keep them all straight. Everything is a sin to somebody's god."

I thought of Madame Stringent as he said this and nodded. "So I've discovered," I replied. "The sad thing is that some fanatics are actually quite smart."

"Well, ignorance and intelligence are not mutually exclusive. Someone can be astute at knowing many things, but the danger often lies in what he chooses not to know."

"But surely someone can never know everything."

"This is correct. However, one must always be aware of how much he does not know and be both open to and willing to learn new points of view.

"In addition," the old man continued, "one must never become haughty and overconfident in his knowledge, for there is always more to learn, and even the wisest can be wrong. I would rather admit that I do not know something than think I know the answer when I actually do not. Come, I want to show you something."

I rose from my chair and followed him to the back wall, which was covered in a large mural. Rows and rows of hand-painted text lined the wall, the words small and neat. I stepped closer to view the inscriptions while the old man continued.

"These are the *Can-Evers,* an ancient text that has been passed down through generations. They consist of sixty-two questions, some easily answered, others less so. There are some can-evers for which no answer is known to man or alien alive."

Can a reflection ever be clearer than the reality it reflects?
Can a pathway ever hide the many points it intersects?
Can a map ever bring guidance to the ones it misdirects?
Can a compass ever be the cause the guide overcorrects?
Can a crossroad ever lose the travelers that it redirects?
Can a purpose ever steer the many goals that it deflects?
Can a tongue ever be silenced by the words that it projects?
Can a message ever stay the same through each voice that inflects?
Can a word ever be altered by the ear that it affects?
Can a thought ever look deep into the one who introspects?
Can a moment ever linger for a man who disconnects?
Can a leader ever follow after soldiers he directs?
Can a teacher ever learn more than the students he corrects?
Can a thief ever be taken by the things that he collects?
Can the law ever commit the very crime that it detects?
Can a traitor ever be betrayed by those whom he defects?
Can a king ever be crowned by citizens that he elects?
Can a writer ever own the story that he codirects?
Can a miner ever have sufficient gold that he prospects?
Can a scientist ever bring life to corpses he prosects?
Can a surgeon ever heal the many tissues he resects?
Can a doctor ever cure himself of sickness he exsects?
Can a mother ever hate the very children she protects?

Can a child ever love the parents that he disrespects?
Can a care ever be cared for by a person who neglects?
Can a hunger ever thirst for just one moment that refects?
Can a mystery ever be unsolved by details it complects?
Can a stinger ever prick the very poison it ejects?
Can a needle ever pierce the very healing it injects?
Can a half ever become a whole through lines that it bisects?
Can a part ever become a full through methods it dissects?
Can a unit ever break into the pieces it confects?
Can a bond ever be torn apart after it reconnects?
Can an honor ever need the many statues it erects?
Can a treasure ever find a man whom it overprotects?
Can a loyalty ever be strong for one who disaffects?
Can a faith ever be lost in one whom everyone respects?
Can a filth ever be purified by cleanness it infects?
Can a soap ever be soiled by the dirt it disinfects?
Can a germ ever be sullied further as it reinfects?
Can a change ever be unchanged by the change that it effects?
Can a choice ever be chosen by the chooser it selects?
Can a voice ever respond back to itself that it objects?
Can a question ever state the very thing it interjects?
Can a memory ever fade away before it recollects?
Can a feeling ever know the ways that it interconnects?
Can a plan ever be scheming up a ploy it architects?
Can a storm ever be calmer than the stillness it disjects?
Can a moon ever be darkened by the beam that it trajects?
Can a sun ever be colder than the heat that it convects?
Can a psyche ever claim to know the reason it cathects?
Can a brain ever defend itself from when it introjects?
Can an ego ever grovel to the knee that genuflects?
Can a life ever attain the form that its own mind perfects?
Can a joy ever be tainted by a moment that dejects?
Can a hope ever be shattered by the dream that it expects?
Can a will ever be broken by the hardness it subjects?
Can a spirit ever die a death after it resurrects?
Can a mind ever be studied more than that which it inspects?

Can a soul ever be trusted by the one that it suspects?
Can a heart ever be welcomed by the thing that it rejects?
Can a love ever be severed by the hearts that it connects?

"I read these often," the old man continued. "They remind me of how much I have yet to know. This is important as you grow wiser. You must always maintain perspective on your knowledge."

I nodded, still staring at the ancient text in awe, my brain trying to answer some of the questions.

"Do you see this chair you were just sitting in?" the old man asked, interrupting my reverie.

I turned around and looked. "Of course," I replied.

"But do you *really* see it?" the man continued. "Strictly speaking, you only see one half of the chair. I can see parts of this chair from my vantage point that you cannot, and there are other parts still that only someone standing at the other end of the room would see."

Illustrating his point, the old man paced the room, surveying the chair from every conceivable angle before resuming his thought. "Everything you see, you only see half of it. For everything you stare at, everything you think is so clear, as much as you see, there's at least as much that you don't. This is why it is important to always be learning, never content in what you already know."

"I see," I replied, intrigued by the man's explanation. The Vream indeed seemed quite wise, and I wanted to learn more.

As if sensing my curiosity, the old man turned to me and said with a smile, "Please don't hesitate to ask questions if you have them. Questions are the fuel that keeps the fires of conversation burning."

"Some questions cannot be answered," I noted wryly, gesturing toward the mural.

The old man acknowledged my statement with a nod. "This is true," he responded, before breaking into verse:

There'll always be someone to answer you
When you ask the questions "What?" or "Who?"
And always there'll be someone standing there
To answer "When?" or show you "How?" or tell you "Where?"
But we will carry with us till we die,
Never answered, the immortal question, "Why?"

"So you're a poet?" I asked.

"I dabble here and there. Thoughts and ideas are not limited to the prose form. Sometimes, the best way to express something is with a poem."

"I like poetry too. Haven't written anything in a while though."

"Well, when this adventure is over, maybe you'll find the time to try again."

"Maybe. So far, I feel like this trip I've been on has just filled my head with a lot of useless information."

"Now, now," the old man countered. "There is no such thing as useless information…only information without context, which life will provide in due time."

"Huh. Hadn't thought about it that way before. Well, even so, I hope this quest pays off in the end. It's been quite a ride."

"I hope so as well, for your sake. However, I also hope you find merit in the journey itself, even if the end is not what you hoped it would be. You cannot judge the value of the journey by the destination you end up reaching."

"I suppose not. But I really do hope my journey ends in success. I'm not sure what I'll do otherwise."

"Will you return home after all this is finished?"

"I don't know. There have been times when all I've wanted to do is go home. But then I think of the boredom I felt there, and I wonder if I really want to go back to that. On the other hand, once my quest is complete, my purpose here is done, so why would I stay?"

"These are tough questions indeed. But I have learned a long time ago that the things that bring you here don't have to be the things that keep you here. I am certainly not the same man I was when I first moved to this place, and I have stayed for different reasons than those for which I came."

"Maybe I'll let the universe decide."

"If that is your motto, just remember: you are part of the universe."

"I am, aren't I?" I smiled as I considered this perspective for the first time.

I was in awe of the Vream's seemingly endless wisdom, but a part of me wondered if he was happy with his current situation. Living alone seemed like it could get boring pretty quickly. I decided to probe further.

"Is it hard to live alone?" I asked. "How do you keep from being bored? Or even lonely?"

The old man smiled slightly. "Talk to a man," he said slowly, measuring each word, "and you give him a friend for a day. Teach a man to talk to himself and you give him a friend for a lifetime."

I stood silent for a moment, unsure if he was serious. "Have you always lived alone?" I finally ventured.

A cloud passed over the old man's face. "No, I haven't," he said softly. "I lived with my dear wife, Elizabeth, for years before the gruentia plague took her."

"I'm so sorry to hear that."

"Thank you. I think of her often. I've tried to memorialize her in my poetry, but I can never find the right words."

With this, the old man walked over to a shelf in the corner and retrieved a small wooden chest. After setting it on the table, he opened it and removed a yellowed sheet of paper, which he handed to me. "Here is the latest version my weak brain has attempted."

I took the paper from his trembling fingers and began to read the handwritten poem. It was titled "Sonnet 51 ('Sonnet for Elizabeth')."

I stand out in the woods and breathe a sigh
  As gentle winds caress the autumn leaves
  And all the trees sway gently in the breeze;
I wonder why such beauty has to die.
My thoughts go where Elizabeth does lie,
  Unmoving by the sugar maple trees,
  Where many lips are still and no eye sees—
A place where stony guards can't answer why.

And as the night begins to conquer day,
  In twilight still, I cry, "Elizabeth!
If your cold lips could speak, what would they say?
  What words were sealed forever in your death?
And did those silent lips—somehow, someway—
  Kiss sweet eternal life with their last breath?"

"This is absolutely beautiful," I said, my voice barely above a whisper. "I can feel the love you have for your wife in these words."

"Thank you," the old man replied, his voice choking up with emotion. A single tear slid down his cheek, and he quickly brushed it away. "I'm so sorry. You are a guest in my home. You shouldn't see my sorrow."

"Don't be sorry," I stopped him. "One should never have to apologize for sadness."

The irony of my words did not escape me, given the source of my recent conflict with the Maryvillians, but they seemed like the right words to say in the moment. Besides, I think I really started to believe those words even as I said them. I knew that this man's sadness was vastly different from the one that ruled the nearby village, born out of a deep and undying love for a woman he knew well for many years. But I also knew that sorrow was a complex emotion, and I was starting to wonder if perhaps it was not up to me to judge the nature or merit of another's grief.

Oblivious to my conflicted thoughts, the old man looked at me gratefully. "You are very kind," he said quietly.

As we continued talking into the night, I was struck with the notion to test the old man's wisdom further.

"What is the meaning of life?" I asked, seizing the opportunity. If anyone would know, I felt that he would.

The old man paused and stroked his beard thoughtfully. "Perhaps," he said at length, "perhaps that is the wrong question. Maybe life is not meant to be defined. Maybe life is just meant to be...lived."

"So what's the best way to live it, do you think?"

"Now *that* is the real question. What I have learned in my many years are three things. One: never speak ill of a day before it arrives. Two: make the most of today, for today is yesterday's future. And three: live your life as if yesterday never happened and as though tomorrow may never come; otherwise, one day you may wake up and discover that tomorrow came yesterday and you let it go."

"That's good advice," I remarked. "People are always telling me I should live in the moment."

"And so you should. Live in the moment, in the present, in the now. Be neither paralyzed by the past nor fearful of the future."

"That's tough when you're my age and you have your whole life ahead of you."

"Plan for the future, but don't be ensnared by it. After all, the future is just made up of many little 'presents' following each other, one moment after another."

"I just want to make sure I make the right choices. I don't want to do anything that's going to hurt or scar me."

"Pain is, unfortunately, an unavoidable companion to life. We can hide from it, but it will always find us."

"So what can you do?"

"Don't be so afraid of scars. Scars are wounds that have healed."

I pondered his words before replying. "I hadn't thought of them that way before, but I suppose you're right."

We sat in silence for a brief moment.

"And now," the old man said, beginning to pace the floor, "let me ask *you* a question. Which is better: having unsatisfied desire or having something you can never fully appreciate?"

"Hmm, that's a tough one." I squinted my eyes in concentration. "Give me an example."

"Money. Unfortunately, they do not call me a miser for nothing. I have much gold that I've hoarded over the years, but the more I gain, the more I seem to desire."

I was more than a little surprised to learn this, given the humble surroundings the old man lived in. Regardless, I forced myself to focus on the question at hand.

"It sounds like you have both problems," I replied after a moment's deliberation. "Your desire for gold is always unsatiated, and you can't appreciate the wealth you have already accumulated."

"The miser's curse indeed. Any words of advice for me?"

I paused for another moment, surprised that the old man would seek my wisdom. After a while, I responded tentatively. "Well, all I can say is that it seems that money's true purpose is to be spent."

The old man nodded. "Go on."

"Why do we save money? To spend it later. Why do we pass it down to our children? So they can spend it. Why do we give money to charity? So others can spend it. The chief end of money is to be spent."

The old man looked at me in amazement. "Words so wise from someone so young," he mused quietly to himself. "I will take those words to heart."

π π π π π

The two of us continued talking through the night. One of the many topics we discussed was the strange and mournful culture of Maryville.

"I actually pity the residents of Maryville," the old man said. "They are trapped in a cycle of sorrow with no escape.

Their devotion to this Mary woman has turned fanatical and even dangerous."

"It reminds me of these women back on X@X," I said, thinking of Madame Stringent, Greta, and Gretchen. "They are always obsessively grieving over various 'sins' that they find in others."

"The act of finding faults in others is a fault in itself," the old man pointed out.

I nodded in agreement. "I think they are realizing that the universe is changing, and they are becoming more desperate to preserve their way of life. They're always casting blame on others."

"A desperate person will always find something to blame," the old man noted.

"Ain't that the truth," I agreed, glancing down at a beam of light stretching itself out on the floor in front of me. To my surprise, the sun had risen over the forest, its rays streaming in through the single window in the Vream's hut.

"Well, I suppose that's my cue to go," I said. "Much as I'd like to stay, my friend Qarl needs my help."

"Yes, indeed," the old man replied. "If I know the Maryvillians, Qarl is undergoing indoctrination as we speak. But worry not. In the village beyond these woods is an alien lawyer named Travvis Trothers. He is a good friend of mine and can help get your friend out of trouble. He grew up in Maryville and knows many of the people on the council. Tell him the Wiser Miser sent you."

"Will do. Thank you so much for your help and advice."

"It has been my pleasure, but do tread carefully. Advice can be misleading, you know."

Chapter M

I left the Vream's home and made my way through the woods to the next town. After asking around for where I might find Travvis the lawyer, I was directed to a large building in the center of town.

Once inside, I approached the secretary and informed her of who I was looking for. Travvis was out at the moment, I was told, and would be back shortly. I was invited to sit in the lounge down the hall while I waited.

On my way to the lounge, I was detoured by the sound of muffled arguing. I followed the voices down the other end of the hall to a large conference room. Peering into the room, I was intrigued by what I saw.

Two tall aliens in business suits were arguing vehemently, gesturing toward a giant whiteboard as they spoke. A riddle was written on the board, one I instantly recognized as a popular brain teaser back on Earth. It went something like this:

A, **B**, and **C** are traveling through a desert together. While at an oasis, **A** and **B** each decide separately to kill **C**. **A** poisons **C**'s canteen, and, later, **B** drains it. **C** dies of thirst. Who killed **C**: **A** or **B**?

"The murderer is most obviously **B**," the alien on the left was saying.

"I disagree," replied the alien on the right. "**A** is the murderer. After all, he was the one who put a lethal substance into **C**'s canteen."

"But **C** did not die from the poison," countered the first alien. "He died of thirst, which was brought on by **B** draining the canteen. **B** is most definitely the murderer here."

"Indeed, thirst was the actual cause of death," the second alien replied. "But **A** did not know that **B** would drain the canteen. Had **B** not done so, **A**'s poison would have certainly killed **C** directly. In other words, **C** would not be any less dead if **B** had decided to leave the canteen alone. **A**'s intent was murder the entire time, and he initiated the crime; his specific method just happened to be preempted by **B**'s method. I say **A** is guilty."

"Intent does not equal execution," the first alien countered again. "The fact that **A** intended to murder **C** does not mean that he actually did. **A** may have been unaware that **B** would drain the canteen and foil his plan, but the fact remains that **B** *did* drain the canteen, which directly resulted in **C**'s death by thirst. **B** is guilty."

"But **A**'s plan would have worked perfectly. If **B** had not intervened, **C** would still be dead right now, only via poison."

"**B**'s method would have worked either way, *regardless* of **A**'s scheming. See, no matter what **A** did or didn't do, **B**'s actions would have ended in the same result. Whether it was water or poison he drained out of that canteen, he still would've effectively caused **C**'s death by thirst."

"But that's just it: *because* **A** poisoned the canteen, **B** was no longer draining out anything that was life-giving or thirst-quenching from that canteen. **B** may as well have been dumping sand out of it, because **A** had tainted it. It was **A** who negated the quality of **C**'s water, and it was **A** who deprived **C** of life-giving liquid, so ultimately **A** is responsible for the murder."

"That doesn't matter. The cause of death was *thirst*. It was **B** who emptied the canteen. So **B** is guilty. Simple as that."

"You're overlooking the fact that **A** still could've caused a death by thirst. The instant he poisoned that canteen, **C** was no longer in possession of something good to quench his thirst with, even though the liquid was still technically floating in his canteen. In fact, had **C** discovered that there was poison in his canteen before **B** drained it, he would've had to throw away his tainted water himself, and guess how he would have died? Thirst!"

"But we'll never know that for sure, will we, since **B** was the one who *actually* drained the canteen."

The alien on the right had his mouth open to respond, but I had had enough of the bickering. The answer was so obvious to me. Stepping forward into the room, I cleared my throat loudly.

"You're both wrong," I stated emphatically.

The suited aliens turned and stared at me, their narrow eyes unblinking, no doubt wondering what the hell I was doing there. Finally the one on the left spoke.

"How could we both be wrong?"

"Precisely," the other one chimed in. "What are you trying to say? That both of them are equally culpable in this murder?"

I shook my head. "Nope. Neither of them are. The killer wasn't **A** *or* **B**."

Their eyes bulged slightly in incredulity. "Who, then?" they asked in unison.

"It was **C**," I replied matter-of-factly. "**C** killed himself." Stepping between them, I tapped at the writing on the board. "They were at a desert oasis. Why didn't **C** just refill his canteen?"

You could've heard a pin drop as this perspective sank in. The two aliens stared at the board, motionless, while I stood back and grinned, feeling rather proud of myself.

"Why didn't we consider that option before?" the left alien pondered, his brow furrowed.

"I don't know," the right alien responded, "but this changes everything."

"So what's up with the riddle, guys?" I asked. "Is this like a logic class or something?" I peered around the room, looking for students of some sort. The aliens turned and looked at me oddly.

"We're lawyers," the one on the right huffed. "And who exactly are you?"

"Oh, I'm just an Earth-human. I'm waiting for Travvis. Don't mind me." I grinned at them, still feeling a bit cocky. "So this must be like a training exercise for you, huh?"

The alien on the left shook his head. "No, this is a real case. Someone was killed in the Dezert of Dan recently, and his two companions were placed on trial for murder. We were their attorneys. The trial is over, but my opponent and I are still bickering over the case."

"So if the trial is over, who was found guilty?" I asked.

"They both were," the alien on the right replied. "They are supposed to be executed today." He paused for a moment, then jumped forward with a start as the realization hit him. "*TODAY!!!*" he shouted, his eyes wide.

"Today!" the alien on the left repeated, arriving at the same thought simultaneously. "But they're both innocent!"

"I know that!" the right alien shouted back. "We have to stop the execution."

"Let's go, then!" the left alien said emphatically, rushing out the door and down the hall, his opponent right behind him.

I stood alone in the room, startled for a moment, my mind processing what had just happened. *This is real!* I thought. *This isn't a riddle. These are real lives at stake…and you just saved them.*

Or maybe I hadn't. Maybe it was too late. I had to make sure! I turned on my heel, dashed out the door, and ran to catch up with the lawyers.

"What's going to happen to them?" I hollered as I finally overtook the running aliens in the hallway.

"They have been sentenced to death by sweet nothings!" one of them replied, panting as he spoke.

"What the hell is that?" I asked, struggling to keep up with the attorneys as we rounded a corner.

"It is a terrible death," the other replied. "They whisper sweet nothings in your ear, and then…then…oh, it's too horrific to describe!"

Sweat poured down his face as he quickened his pace and his companion did likewise. I increased my stride to match theirs, intent on helping them halt the execution at all costs. I had forgotten all about finding Travvis and rescuing Qarl at that point.

We raced through hallways and around corners—the two lawyers chiding themselves in frantic mutters for being so stupid—and finally screeched to a halt before a large window.

Behind the glass was a small room painted entirely in white and bathed in harsh fluorescent light from lamps along the ceiling. In the center of the room sat two large chairs. An alien was seated in each, straps around their wrists, ankles, and chest holding them in place. A large metal box with blinking lights stood beside each chair, and from the side of each box extended a long, snaking hose, which attached to a funnel that was placed directly against the ear of the alien in the chair. A similar hose coiled out the opposite end of each box, ending in what looked to be a rudimentary mouthpiece.

Besides the two prisoners in the chairs, two other aliens dressed entirely in black occupied the room. One stood in the corner, solemnly observing the proceedings, while the other rolled around on a wheeled stool, checking the strange equipment and ensuring that the convicts were secured in their seats.

The two aliens overseeing the execution were quite terrifying to behold. Their upper bodies were humanlike in appearance, but from the waist down they sported twitching black tentacles instead of legs. They were dressed in black hooded tunics with long sleeves that covered their hands. Their hoods were worn up over their heads, and, despite the bright light in the room, not a trace of their faces could be seen from the shadows cast by the hoods. It was as if soulless beings occupied those clothes.

But perhaps executioners couldn't afford to have souls.

Once his checks were complete, the alien on the stool glanced at the one in the corner, who nodded for him to continue. Propelling himself with his unnerving tentacles, the first alien glided his stool across the floor until he had positioned himself beside the mouthpiece of the box by the prisoner on the right.

I was jolted from the spectacle by the two attorneys, who had leapt forward and begun pounding on the window. Realizing the urgency of the situation, I joined them in assaulting the heavy glass, desperate to stop whatever horror was about to ensue. To my surprise, no one in the room even flinched.

The seated executioner slowly and methodically reached up to flip a switch on the box while his companion continued to watch. The lights on the metal device responded by changing color and blinking faster. The prisoners continued to sit motionless, resigned to their fate.

"What's wrong with them!?!" I shouted to the two lawyers, my fists aching from striking the thick pane. "Are they ignoring us?" I hit the window harder and harder, but the occupants of the room seemed oblivious to our presence.

"It's no use," one lawyer replied in frustration as he ceased his pounding. "They can't hear us. It's soundproof glass."

"But why aren't they even acknowledging us?" I asked incredulously. I began hopping up and down before the window, waving my arms in a futile attempt to attract attention. No one in the room seemed to notice.

"This must be a one-way mirror," the other lawyer replied, examining the glass. "They must've installed this so that executions could be watched without anyone disturbing the executioners. Public outdoor executions haven't gone so well in the past."

"Well, we can't just stand here!" I interjected. "We've got to do something! Where's the door to this room?"

I looked around desperately for a way in, but the window appeared to be the only opening. Meanwhile, inside the room of death, the executioner was reaching up to adjust his mouthpiece.

"I don't think there is a door," the first lawyer told me. "The prison is underground, so prisoners are usually brought up onto this level through trapdoors. It's for security purposes. During trials, they are brought up through a trapdoor into a doorless cage in the courtroom, and I'm guessing this room operates the same way…to keep anyone from breaking in or out."

"You *guess*?" I repeated, my voice filled with shocked disbelief. "You two don't seem to know this place very well."

"Well, we're kinda new," the second lawyer admitted, a sheepish look on his face.

"Clearly," I quipped sarcastically. Turning my attention back to the events taking place in the room, I realized that time was running out. The seated executioner had finished his adjustments and was leaning slowly toward the mouthpiece.

"He's going to do it!" squeaked the first lawyer. "He's going to whisper the sweet nothings!"

"Oh, I can't watch!" wailed the second lawyer, turning away and hiding his face in his hands.

I grabbed the two attorneys and shook them violently. "We *have* to stop this execution!" I shouted. "Quick, go find something to break the window. I'll keep trying to get their attention."

Both lawyers raced around the corner in search of objects to hurl at the glass, while I turned my attention back to the proceedings within the room. I had raised my fists to resume my pounding when I became transfixed by the happenings beyond the window.

And what I witnessed chilled me to the core.

The seated executioner had positioned the mouthpiece directly in front of the dark void that was his face. He leaned forward as if to speak into it, and I felt a sudden shiver travel down my spine. I couldn't hear a sound due to the thick glass in between us, and I couldn't see his lips move because of the dark hood, but I knew he was speaking…whispering…saying *something* into that mouthpiece. The connecting hose trembled slightly, and the lights on the metal box transformed their blinking into a steady, menacing glow.

As I watched in frozen horror, the prisoner on the right began to shake. The trembling began slowly at first, then rapidly increased in intensity until he was shuddering violently. The executioner slowly leaned back from the mouthpiece, his dreadful whisperings complete, and glided his chair away to join his companion in the corner. I instinctively took a step back from the window as well, unsure of what to expect.

The prisoner continued to shake intensely, his body straining against the bonds as it thrashed with involuntary convulsions. The metal box's lights continued to glow steadily. The hose connected to the earpiece funnel vibrated as the device kept transmitting the cryptic whisperings of the executioner to the helpless prisoner's ear. And then, before my eyes, his appearance began to change.

In utter disbelief, I watched as the skin around the prisoner's arms and legs began to contract until I could see the outline of every bone, vein, and muscle. His chest and abdomen proceeded to cave in, exposing every rib and organ. I continued to gaze in horror as his cheeks and eye sockets sank in deeply, causing his eyes to bulge out dramatically. It was as if the sounds entering the convict's ear were literally sucking the life out of him!

The alien prisoner's green blood began to trickle from every orifice as he continued to convulse from the merciless force within his body. His mouth was stretched open in a silent scream, and his protruding, bleeding eyes haunted me with their horrific expression.

Then, in an instant, the pressure overcame the fragile body, and the prisoner imploded violently in a mess of blood and goo, spattering bodily fluids everywhere. I jumped back from the window in shock.

Chapter N

As I continued watching, helplessly hypnotized by the horrifying happenings beyond the window, the executioner glided his stool over to the prisoner on the left. The switch on the metal box was flipped, and the lights on the box began to blink faster. As the executioner reached up to adjust his mouthpiece, the lights on the device suddenly went dark.

The executioner released his hold on the mouthpiece and rose up on his frightening tentacles. He examined the box carefully, looking for the source of the sudden power outage. The other executioner left his post in the corner and joined in the search.

Just then, a circular gap in the floor appeared as a hidden trapdoor was opened. An alien rose through the opening, frantically waving his arms. The executioners swiveled sharply, acknowledging the new presence in the room. As the alien clambered to his feet, he appeared to be speaking, but since his back was to me, I couldn't make out the words.

My attention was interrupted by the return of the two lawyers, who dashed around the corner and screeched to a halt before the window.

"We found Travvis!" the first one panted.

"He's stopping the execution now," gasped the second one, gesturing toward the window as he leaned over to catch his breath.

"I'm afraid he's a little late," I remarked. The two attorneys exchanged dismayed glances as they noticed the gory puddle that was the deceased prisoner.

"Oh dear, oh my, oh goodness!" they muttered hysterically to themselves. They began to pace the floor wildly, bewailing the terrible situation and the end of their careers it was certain to bring.

Ignoring the duo anxiously orbiting the room, I turned back to the proceedings behind the glass. The first executioner was releasing the living prisoner from his bonds, while the second executioner glided over to the corner, retrieved a mop, and began cleaning up the remains of the dead companion.

Travvis shook his head before disappearing back down the trapdoor in the floor. A few moments later, he reappeared around the corner.

Travvis Trothers was a handsome alien, tall and lanky. His skin had a luminescent glow to it, and his hair glittered and sparkled in the light cast off by his skin.

"What the hell happened?" Travvis asked. The two lawyers hung their heads.

"We couldn't figure out how to get in the room," the first one replied.

"We tried breaking the glass," the second one pointed out, as if that revelation would make the situation better.

"Well, it's too late now. We can't undo what's already done. The judge will have a fit though, I'm sure. You two should write a report about what happened."

The two lawyers shuffled their way back down the hall, wringing their hands and casting blame on each other for the whole unfortunate state of affairs. Travvis turned to me.

"Idiots," he remarked with a slight smile. "And who might you be?"

I explained who I was and my current predicament while he listened intently. When I mentioned the Wiser Miser, Travvis's face lit up.

"I miss that guy!" he exclaimed. "How is he doing?"

"He's well," I replied. "Very wise, as I'm sure you know."

"Yes, he's quite a man. I'm glad he sent you to me. I'd be happy to help you and your friend Qarl."

Travvis led me outside to his vehicle. It was a magnificent car, with an aerodynamic, sloping hood in the front and pointed fins in the rear. It had five wheels and a fascinating coat of paint that changed color every minute or so.

"Hop in!" Travvis invited, clapping his hands to open the passenger door, which slid downward and under the car. I complied eagerly.

"Nice ride!" I exclaimed.

"Thank you," Travvis replied with a grin. "It's the latest WheelMobile model, the Hx9. Comes with all the latest features."

"It's amazing."

"I shouldn't brag though. You know what they say: the nicer the vehicle, the bigger the asshole that drives it." He chuckled merrily.

"We say that on Earth too. Still, this is a great vehicle. Qarl would absolutely drool over this."

"Well, the sooner we get your friend back, the sooner he can." Travvis revved the engine. "Let's go!"

With that, we took off down the road toward Maryville. As we drove, I struck up a conversation with my companion.

"So, the Vream—I mean, the Wiser Miser—said you're originally from Maryville?"

"Yes, I was born and raised there."

"Why did you leave?"

"I was actually kicked out by the village council."

"Oh shit, how come?"

"They expelled me for being a gaylien."

"What's a gaylien?"

"We are a rare species of alien. We possess the Jenkins O'Yenkins gene."

"What does the gene do?"

"Several things. For one, it causes us to be much happier than most. You will seldom see a sad gaylien. We also reproduce asexually—TMI, I know—and can see more colors in the light spectrum than any other species."

"That's cool. What colors can you see that we can't?"

"All kinds. Rorange and broink and blurple and bleige and grellow and grold and whilver and vindigo and chartravender and so, so many others."

I was intrigued by the thought of colors that my eyes had never seen. "That's really fascinating! What is it like to see so many colors?"

"Well, to me it's normal, but I love that the universe is so beautiful and colorful. I recognize that what I possess is a gift, and I'm grateful for it."

"So the council didn't like that you were a gaylien?"

"Not at all."

"Why not?"

"I was too different. The worst sin was that I was too happy for them. I couldn't mourn the absence of Mary like everyone else did. Trust me, I tried, but the sorrow just wasn't there. It took me a long time before I found out about the gene I had. Once I knew about it, everything made so much more sense."

He continued, "But the council doesn't believe in the JOY gene. They think I chose to be this way. And so they eventually got rid of me."

I shook my head. "That's terrible."

"Not as terrible as choosing to live a lie would've been. To stifle my natural joy would've been torture. Trust me, I know from experience."

"I imagine it was hard growing up in such an environment."

"At times it was very difficult. There were moments when I hated who I was and wished I could be like everyone else. The constant urge I felt to be joyful was exhausting to fight. I eventually couldn't do it anymore.

"I began to let myself feel happy, although I was careful not to express it around others. The council caught on, however, and that was my cue to exit. I've never felt more free though. I can't imagine going back now."

We continued driving in silence as I pondered the implications of being raised as Travvis had been. I couldn't imagine having to be untrue to myself for so many years, enduring the fact that the alternative to inner conflict and pain was loss and rejection. Thinking about Travvis's long and difficult journey of self-discovery, I was moved by his fearlessness and fierce insistence on being himself, regardless of the consequences.

"So, what prompted you to pursue law?" I ventured at length.

"I wanted to fight for gaylien rights and ensure that no one else go through what I went through. The battle isn't over yet, but strides have been made."

"You must be very busy."

"I am. I'm a lawyer by day, and, by night, I work with a team of gayliens on designing the Colorplex."

"What's the Colorplex?"

"It's a virtual reality experience, a tour that uses state-of-the-art NueTrueHueVue™ technology to simulate how gayliens see. We hope to give visitors a chance to see through the eyes of a gaylien and, in the process, learn about our history and our ongoing struggle for equality."

"That sounds amazing. I'd love to visit the Colorplex once it's finished."

"We'd love to have you! You'll get to see all the cool colors that I see every day."

The two of us continued chatting as we drove. It wasn't long before we entered Maryville. Travvis pulled up in front of the council hall. Brooding and familiar, the ominous gray building forboded the ugly confrontation we were about to have inside its walls. I shivered nervously in dreaded anticipation.

We exited the Hx9 and walked silently up the steps and into the building. A secretary tried to stop us in the lobby, but Travvis pushed past her, waving his credentials before making his way to the council chambers.

What I saw inside was startling.

Qarl was seated in a plain metal chair. He was wearing a silver helmet, from which a flexible arm protruded. Attached to the arm was a screen that was positioned directly in front of Qarl's eyes. Dark and sad images flashed on the screen as Qarl sat, catatonic, tears streaming down his face. Two speakers within the helmet blared mournful music into his ears, the notes synchronizing perfectly with the images.

The judge who had banished me and a few guards were hovering around Qarl as he underwent his indoctrination. Everyone looked up with startled expressions as we barged into the room. A shadow passed over the judge's face when she saw Travvis, and her omnipresent cloud darkened.

"What are you doing here?" the judge questioned coldly. "Go away. I do not wish to see you."

"Turn off the Indoctribot," Travvis replied. "You can't keep Qarl here."

"He is here willingly," the judge retorted.

"He's clearly under the influence. He has no will of his own at this point."

"He is one of ours now and shall add his sorrow to our own. Perhaps his grief shall be the one to bring Mary back."

"Mother, please stop," Travvis said gently. A silence fell over the chamber. I couldn't believe my ears.

"Don't call me that!" the judge scolded. "You are no longer my son. You have chosen a life that is contrary to our ways."

"Mother, it's me. Please listen."

"I know what you are doing. Appealing to motherhood will not help your case."

"Hasn't there been enough hurt in this village? Enough rejection? Why separate this man from his friend?"

"We need him. We need Mary to return. She sees that there is not enough sorrow, and she is staying away." Her voice faltered as she said this. "I have dedicated my life to bringing Mary back, and I cannot fail now."

"Maybe it's time to let go."

Mother Trothers shook her head silently, as if she was wrestling with the decision. Finally she spoke.

"Turn off the Indoctribot," she said quietly. The guards complied with her order, and Qarl staggered over to us.

"Leave at once, before I change my mind," Mother said coldly to Travvis. "And do not show your face here ever again."

With that, she turned on her heel and exited the room, her guards following suit. I caught a glimpse of her face as she left. It was wet, whether with actual tears or with drops from the cloud above her head, I couldn't tell, but I wanted to believe that she was mourning something important for once: that her son was walking out of her life, perhaps for the last time.

We wasted no time in getting Qarl out of the council hall and into the Hx9. After dumping Qarl in the backseat, Travvis and I hopped in and were quickly on our way out of Maryville.

We rode in silence for a while, the gravity of what had just occurred hanging over me like a thick blanket. After a time, I spoke up tentatively.

"I didn't know she was your mother," I said, unsure of what to say.

"Yep," Travvis replied. "Charming, isn't she?"

"That was horrible, the way she rejected you."

"Yes, it is, but, unfortunately, I'm used to it. This isn't the first confrontation we've had that's ended this way."

"Well, all I can say is I'm sorry."

"Thanks, buddy. Everything will be ok. If they can't stand my happiness, that's their loss."

I glanced toward the backseat to check on Qarl. He was slumped over, staring off into space, his cheeks still wet with tears. It was surreal to see him in this state, eerily silent and too sorrowful to even enjoy the magnificent vehicle he was riding in.

"A fair warning," Travvis pointed out. "It may take some time for Qarl to recover from the indoctrination he underwent. He's likely to be in, shall we say, a mournful mood for a bit."

We parked in the woods near the Vream's residence. Qarl planted himself by a giant tree and refused to go any farther until he had taken a nap. He curled up beneath the tree, next to a tall green plant, and went right to sleep. As he slept, I stayed with him while Travvis ran over to the Vream's place for a quick hello.

With Travvis gone and Qarl fast asleep, I took the time to collect my thoughts. There had been much of late that had detoured me and the group, but the Queen's quest still hung in the back of my mind. The meeting with Asdf and Jkl would be occurring soon, and I knew that the fate of many aliens and humans rested upon my powers of persuasion.

I paced the forest floor, back and forth, mentally constructing my speech to the Great Leaders. Knowing how crucial it was that I neither say nor do anything that might provoke their displeasure, I thought each word and mannerism through carefully, discarding any that could be construed as presumptuous or disrespectful.

Qarl began to stir, his catnap coming to a close. I rushed over to him, eager to see if he had fully recovered from his doleful state.

Alas, he had not.

Upon awaking, Qarl discovered that he had rolled onto the plant during his slumber and crushed it to death. He immediately began sobbing. When I asked what was wrong, he gestured to the plant while blubbering incoherently. I looked around for Travvis, unsure of what to do. I had dealt with displeased Qarl, delirious Qarl, and drunk Qarl, but I wasn't prepared to handle depressed Qarl.

Qarl eventually fell silent, observing the mutilated plant before him solemnly. After a few minutes, he knelt before the mangled foliage, expelled a woeful sigh, and began speaking in verse:

Farewell to thee, thou dearest of all plants,
Which wert, short time ago, a fairest dream,
But now, whether by Fate or merely chance,
Art robbed of Life's minutest spark or gleam.

It seemeth strange that thou wert once so tall,
So full of life, so strong, and, oh, so green,
When now a frail and wilted thing is all
That in this tragic moment can be seen.

Where art thou now, fair jewel of the wood?
Art thou forever gone from Time and Space?
Dost thou lie here where once in life thou stood,
Or in some sweet, ethereal resting place?

Recall I well thy last few hours of life—
A mirror of thy existence overall;
How hard thou fought, through pain and toil and strife!
Alas! At last thou finally hadst to fall.

Thy withered leaves and drooping stem now speak
A strong and silent message from the grave:
In life, fight on, although the way be bleak;
In death, be strong, have courage, and be brave!

Farewell, thou beauteous flower of the wild!
It is with sorrow that I turn away.
But by thy death, the grown one and the child
Shalt find the strength to fight another day!

Travvis returned just as Qarl was finishing up the last stanza. I updated him on Qarl's current state and was assured that a poetic outburst was normal during the recovery process.

"It'll be ok, little buddy," Travvis told Qarl, patting him on the back. "Just let it all out, and you'll feel as good as new shortly."

Now that Qarl was taken care of, my thoughts turned back to the mission at hand. "How are we going to find the Queen and the rest?" I worried aloud.

"I'll send up a rednif," Travvis replied. "It should be able to locate your party."

He took a device out of his pocket and punched a few numbers on the keypad. Within seconds, a screech was heard overhead. A beautiful red bird landed on Travvis's arm. Travvis whispered a few words to the rednif, and it took off again with another screech.

"Give her a few minutes," Travvis instructed. "She'll locate them soon."

A few minutes later, his device beeped, and coordinates popped up on the screen.

"Your party is near Pashko's Pond," Travvis announced. "That is not far from here." He gave me clear instructions on how to reach the pond.

Bidding Travvis goodbye and thanking him for his help, Qarl and I journeyed to Pashko's Pond without incident. It wasn't long before I caught a glimpse of the Queen's purple cape and Bobby's blue cap in the distance. The group was huddled around the edge of the pond, staring into the water. I ran to greet them, eager to tell them about my recent adventures and misadventures.

By the time we rejoined the others, Qarl was back to his usual, obnoxious self. He greeted the others jovially and seemed not to remember his brief indoctrination in Maryville. I tactfully chose not to bring it up in front of him.

The Queen appeared especially pleased by our safe arrival. I could see the concern in her eyes melting away as we assured her that we were ok.

"I wish this Travvis had come with you," she said. "I should like to reward him for his kind efforts."

"We'll have to find him on our way back," Bobby spoke up. "He deserves our thanks at the very least."

"I'm so glad you guys are ok!" Tippers said, putting her arm around me. "We were so worried. We looked everywhere for you!"

Quadrell said nothing, but his eyes turned a baby blue, which I interpreted as relief at our return. I nodded at him, and he smiled in reply.

"So what are we all looking at?" I asked, glancing down into the murky waters of the pond. A group of frogs lounging on lily pads met my eyes.

"These fascinating frogs," Bobby replied. To my surprise, the entire assembly of frogs spoke up in unison.

"We are the Freckled Fraternity of the Freethinking Frogs," they croaked. I jumped back, startled. Bobby laughed at me.

As I reapproached, I took a closer look at the frogs. Each one occupied its own lily pad, drifting lazily at the water's edge. The frogs were your typical green, but each had a black freckle painted on its back. A giant bullfrog floated in the center of the group. His bulging eyes met mine, and he seemed to read my quizzical gaze.

"The freckle is our emblem," the bullfrog explained. "Each one is unique and independent. And thus are we: free in thought and autonomous in society, not bound by ruler nor religion. Reason and logic are our guides to the truth in this universe.

"We are not like the birds," he continued, "who preen themselves haughtily to impress others. We are not like the fish, who travel in schools, incapable of independent decision. Nay, we are free in body and mind. Our aim is neither to be special nor to conform to others, but to be truthful."

"If we be deemed unbecoming in our appearance, so be it," spoke up another frog. "Tell me, would we appreciate beauty if everything were beautiful?"

"And if we be deemed average in our conduct, so be it," another frog chimed in. "Without average, who's to know what is extraordinary and what is dull?" Without missing a beat, his long pink tongue flew out of his mouth and captured a mosquito buzzing by my ear. I jumped, and Bobby laughed again.

"You are an Earth-human, are you not?" the bullfrog leader addressed me directly.

"I am."

"Tell me, why do you Earth-humans like to say, 'Fall seven times, get up eight'? That makes no sense. How can you get up an eighth time if you haven't fallen an eighth time?"

I shrugged. "I don't know."

"I suppose the only way this would work," spoke up a small frog timidly, "is if you started on the ground and got up one time without falling first."

"Ah, this is true," agreed the bullfrog. "Good thinking, young one." The younger frog croaked happily at the affirmation.

Turning to me again, the bullfrog continued. "I couldn't help overhearing earlier that you spent some time in Maryville."

"I did."

"Tell me, how did you find their way of life?"

"Confusing…strict…sad."

"It is all that and more," the bullfrog declared. "Religion is one of the deadliest poisons ever self-administered by livingkind. It is an enemy of free thought." I was a bit taken aback by his candor but wasn't sure I disagreed.

The bullfrog wasn't finished. "Absolute authority is another foe of the mind. Why do we need the rulers of Hob? Why do we need a queen? We are capable of governing ourselves."

One of the Queen's soldiers marched over to silence the frog leader, but the Queen stopped him. "Let him speak," she instructed calmly. The soldier backed away. The bullfrog blinked at him before continuing.

"If we do not like our rulers, perhaps the problem is not the choice of ruler, but rather that we are not meant to be ruled. Why trade one master for another?" The Queen listened intently to his words but chose—perhaps wisely—not to engage.

When they weren't zapping flies or bellowing aphorisms, the Freckled Fraternity of the Freethinking Frogs recited a motto amongst themselves with gusto, slapping a rudimentary rhythm on their lily pads as they croaked in unison:

Ribbit, Ribbit
Blind faith prohibit
Ribbit, Ribbit
Free thought exhibit
Ribbit, Ribbit
No mind inhibit
Ribbit, Ribbit

"Do you share your ideals with everyone who passes this way?" I asked the bullfrog leader.

"We have an obligation to," he replied. "There are many ears in this pond and beyond. They all belong to creatures whose minds deserve to be free. We have a responsibility to speak our truth to them. The larger your audience when you speak, the louder your silence when you don't."

Indeed, the frogs' ideas seemed to be spreading around the pond. There was a Sorority of Snails, Snakes, and Snapping Turtles at the other end. One of their rallying cries was "We are so much more than the shells we inhabit!" Made sense. "You have to break the shell to get to the yolk!" was another. That one made less sense. Regardless, it was clear that Pashko's Pond was quite a progressive body of water.

At length, the Queen spoke up. "We have lost too much precious time. We should resume our travels at once."

"The research center should be just ahead," Tippers said. "We'll get there in no time."

With that, our group set off once more.

Chapter 0

Thankfully, nothing more of interest happened before we reached the research center. Soon our group was standing outside our destination, looking up at the facility. Sprawling yet unpretentious, the building had a practical feel to its exterior, with square corners and medium-gray stones comprising its walls.

As we approached the entrance, an automatic door slid open with a quiet hiss. We passed through the doorway and entered a lobby. The room was cold and echoed loudly as our shoes clicked across the marble floor. A high desk sat in the center, but no receptionist could be seen.

"Which way do we go?" I wondered aloud. "All I have is this paper that says 'For Renn 6. Mark as Read.'"

"Do we need to find someone named Renn?" Bobby asked.

"Maybe we need to find a room marked 6," Tippers suggested.

"Here is the building directory," the Queen pointed out, gesturing toward a large sign in the entranceway. "Perhaps we should start our search here."

The sign in front of us listed the various departments in the building: geology, botany, entomology, forensics, cryptography, psychology…*wait a minute.*

"Forensics!" I exclaimed. "That's it! 'For Renn 6' is forensics. We need to go to the forensics department."

I checked the directory for the location: Wing #72, Room #190. We headed off down a long hallway, following helpful signs posted above our heads.

As we walked, I studied the paper in my hands, wondering what the second part meant. Was I supposed to read something? I tried to pay attention to every sign that hung from the walls and ceiling, but most seemed inconsequential.

"Ugh, I'll never figure this out," I complained aloud. "If only I had pressed Jemon-Aye for more details!"

A man passing us in the hallway stopped and turned. "I don't mean to interrupt," he said, "but did I just hear you mention Jemon-Aye?"

"Yes," I answered cautiously, wondering who this stranger was. "Do you know her?"

"I sure do! She's a dear friend of mine." He stuck out his hand. "I'm so sorry, allow me to introduce myself. I'm Markus Redd."

The name sounded oddly familiar to my ears. "Markus Redd, Markus Redd," I said softly to myself, turning the words over on my tongue. Then it hit me.

"'Mark as Read'! Of course!" I exclaimed, my mind putting the final puzzle piece together. "Jemon-Aye said you could help us."

"How can I be of assistance?"

"Well," I began, "my friends and I are on a quest to reach Hob—" The Queen sidled up and placed her hand on my arm before I could say more.

"Our business requires the utmost secrecy," she said to Markus. "Before we continue, can we count on your discretion?"

Markus's eyes grew wide as a wave of startled recognition washed over his face.

"My Queen!" he exclaimed, dropping to one knee. "My sincerest apologies, I did not know you were here."

"Rise, young man," the Queen purred. Markus complied, although his shocked expression remained. "We need your help to reach Hob, but I must know that you can maintain silent lips in regard to our purpose here."

"Your secrets are safe with me," Markus assured the Queen. "How can I help?"

"Jemon-Aye informed us that there is a telepod here and that you are the only one who knows the coordinates to Hob. Can you convey us safely to our destination?"

Markus bowed deeply. "Your Majesty, I am at your service. I will gladly use the telepod to ferry you and your party to Hob."

The Queen smiled gratefully. "Now, we must disguise our true purpose for being here. My presence is sure to draw curious eyes and speculative whispers."

"Why don't I give you a tour of the facility?" Markus suggested. "You're the Queen of the Cosmos. It's only natural that you should want to survey one of the premier scientific research centers in Middle Space. When we are finished with the tour, I can show you to the pod."

"That is an excellent idea. Please proceed."

"Let's begin with the lab. That is right around the corner." As we turned to follow Markus, the Queen pulled me aside and spoke in a low voice.

"After our failure at the Layr, I did not deem it wise to disclose our reason for wanting to reach Hob. Markus seems helpful, but any opinions he may have about the nature of our quest need not hinder us. He only must know where we want to go, not why."

I nodded, fully understanding her reasoning. We rejoined the group before anyone noticed our absence.

Markus led us to the lab, a brightly lit room with white walls and metal workstations. Aliens in lab coats hovered around various beakers and test equipment.

"Careful," I cautioned Qarl with a smirk as he tripped over the SAFETY BEGINS HERE floor mat in the entryway. He rolled his eyes at me and kept walking.

Our tour commenced at one end of the facility and proceeded to the other. I shall spare you all the inconsequential details but will share some of the highlights.

First, there was the lab, where chemists were concocting a new formula for an advanced version of chill-out gas. This new iteration was called CareAir™ and was intended to have longer-lasting effects than its predecessor.

Then there was the man from the mathematics department who insisted that, in Earth-humans, brain was inversely proportional to beauty. "There's even a formula for it," he informed us excitedly. "It's $y = {}^{1}/_{x}$." Incidentally, this was also the formula for representing someone falling in and out of love, he pointed out. After showing us a graph of his equation, the mathematician proudly showcased his array of acute triangles and their not-so-cute counterparts.

There was the seismology department, which was busy tracking a magnitude 7.2 earthquake on a planet in Confined Space.

There was the timeologist who showed us her latest research for moving sideways through time.

There was the culinary sciences department, where chefs from around the universe were participating in a televised contest called *Cheworthy* to see who could concoct the best dish that balanced both taste and nutrition.

There was the psychology department, where we watched through a one-way mirror while a psychologist interviewed a patient.

"How are you feeling today?" the psychologist asked the young woman.

"Not so good," the patient replied, her shoulders slumped. "Unwanted, unloved, unhappy…" Her voice trailed off. "I'm feeling very 'un' today."

The psychologist took notes and passed them to her colleague. Together, they were researching a cure for feeling "un."

The next department particularly piqued my interest: cryptography. The department was housed in a small dimly lit room that was stuffed to the gills with rows of computers and stacks of papers. Aliens sat hunched over screens that flashed cryptic symbols as others pored over papers while scribbling notes furiously. Still others fiddled with gadgets that contained letters and numbers on rotatable wheels.

Markus approached a hunched gray alien and tapped them on the shoulder. The two exchanged a few words before the alien swiveled around to greet us. The creature was old and wrinkled, with two sets of glasses resting on the end of their crooked nose.

"This is Glennifer," Markus said. "They are the best cryptographer on the planet. I work with them often when I need assistance on a case that involves ciphers. I've asked Glennifer to give you a walk-through of one common type of cipher we come across."

Glennifer began their explanation.

"There are two elements to secret messaging: encryption and concealment. Encryption is where you mask your message by turning it into something different.

"One common way is by using a shift cipher. This is where you shift each letter of your message by a specified number of spaces in the alphabet. The shift number is called a key. So, if your key is five, an *A* would be shifted five spaces to either an *F* or a *V*, depending on the direction of your shift.

"Shift direction is referred to by the acronyms FEBS and BEFS: a FEBS cipher utilizes forward encryption–backward solve, while a BEFS cipher uses backward encryption–forward solve.

"Now, the best shift ciphers use a key with multiple numbers, where each letter in your message is shifted by a different number of spaces. A popular key is pi. Using pi as your key means that the first letter would be shifted three spaces, the second letter would be shifted one space, the third letter would be shifted four spaces, and so on."

"That's so cool!" I exclaimed, thoroughly intrigued.

"Indeed, it is," Glennifer acknowledged before continuing. "The second element of secret messaging is concealment. This is where you hide your encrypted message so that others don't even know there is a secret message to find. You could hide it in a photo, a document, or even a book. You could even split up the message and have one letter of it appear after every punctuation mark in the document. There are many ways to conceal an encrypted message."

As Glennifer concluded their explanation, my brain buzzed with the possibilities of my newfound knowledge. I had a few nerdy friends at college I could start exchanging secret messages with. While the tour continued, I began mentally plotting the contents of my first BEFS cipher.

At length, the tour ended, and our group reconvened in the lobby of the facility. I could tell that the Queen was quite impressed by what she had seen.

"Thank you for the tour, Markus," she said gratefully. "I hope to return soon when I have more time to learn more."

Markus bowed. "It has been my pleasure. Now, allow me to show you to the telepod."

Markus took us to a boarded-up closet in a distant wing of the facility. He pulled a key from his pocket, unlocked the door, and pried it open. Inside was a telepod. It looked very much like the one on Qarl's Ken.10, only older and worn. The metal was dull and rusted in places.

"I will enter the coordinates that will teleport you to Hob," Markus explained. "But be careful. The receiving telepod used to be inside their palace courtyard, but Asdf and Jkl may have moved it. There's no telling where you'll step out."

"We'll be careful," Qarl spoke up.

Markus looked around to be sure we hadn't been followed. Assured that we were safe, he clapped twice, and the telepod's panel popped open with a creak. Our group piled in while Markus turned a few dials and punched a few buttons. Bidding us goodbye, he stepped aside, and the panel closed with a groan.

Remembering my previous teleportation trip, I was a bit apprehensive about the sequel. I won't weary you with the details of how the second teleportation went, but I can tell you that it was just as enlightening and disorienting as the first. When we arrived inside the Hob telepod, I managed to stay upright this time but did have to stagger against the wall for support.

Qarl took the lead, motioning us to the back of the pod while he stood by the front panel.

"Keep quiet, everyone," he whispered. "I'm going to see where we are." He clapped his hands softly, and the panel opened up a crack.

Chapter P

Qarl cautiously poked his blue head out of the telepod, scanning from left to right.

"We're in a hallway," he called back softly into the pod, where the rest of us waited with bated breath.

Qarl had just resumed his watch out the pod opening when he saw something that made him pull his head back from the doorway with a jerk. He spun around to face us and flattened himself against the door panel, holding his finger to his lips.

Steps could be heard approaching, marching closer and closer. A shadow crossed the pod opening as a figure passed in front of the door. Our group collectively held its breath. As we listened intently, the steps receded methodically into the distance.

"It's a Hob Goblin!" Qarl hissed once the figure was out of earshot.

"Oh, I've heard about those," Bobby said softly. "They're the soldiers of Hob, aren't they?"

Qarl nodded. "They are nasty creatures that have been bred for the sole purpose of protecting the Great Palace of Hob. It's best that we avoid them."

With the Hob Goblin gone, Qarl peered out the door crack once more. The way was clear, so he slid the panel open and beckoned for us to exit the pod.

We were in a large hallway. A high ceiling loomed above our heads, and tall imposing columns guarded us on either side. Elegant marble floors spanned the entire stretch of hallway in both directions. The windowless space was dim, and the air was dismal and cold, lending the space an uninviting atmosphere.

Qarl motioned for us to follow him as he headed off down the hallway. I wondered how he knew which way to go, but, then again, Qarl did know a lot of things. I figured that he had learned much about Hob in his travels.

We continued walking quietly, trying not to let our shoes clack on the marble floor. Occasionally Qarl would halt us with a wave of his hand and cock his head to listen. Distant steps could sometimes be heard, but no one else entered the hallway.

We eventually rounded a corner and were faced with a pair of large ornate doors. Two Hob Goblins guarded the entryway. They were curious-looking creatures, to be sure: short and squat, almost as wide as they were high, and barely tall enough to pass my waist. Their skin was grayish-brown and lumpy, and multiple eyes were scattered throughout their heads. Random hairs sprouted out from all parts of their bodies. They looked like hairy baked potatoes, to be honest.

Each Goblin wore a belt that held a small dagger, the hilts of which they grasped firmly as we approached, grunting at us to stop.

The Queen took the lead at this point. "We come in peace," she said to the Goblins. "I, the Queen of the Cosmos, and my companion, an Earth-human, request an audience with your masters."

The Goblins grunted amongst themselves for a moment before one of them ducked away through the ornate doors, leaving the other to guard us. A moment later, the first Goblin returned and wordlessly motioned us to follow it.

The Queen gathered us in a quick huddle. "We three will meet with Asdf and Jkl," she said, gesturing at herself, Qarl, and me. "The rest of you, stay out here, and keep watch for any trouble." The others nodded in agreement.

As we turned to enter the throne room, however, Qarl hung back.

"You two go ahead," he said, scratching his horn.

"Is everything all right, Qarl?" the Queen asked gently, concern in her voice.

"Yes," he responded, fidgeting a bit. "I just think I should stay here and keep watch with the others."

"Are you sure? Don't you want to meet the Great Leaders with us?"

"Thank you," he said decisively, "but I'd best hang out here."

"Very well, then," the Queen conceded. "Let me know if there is any trouble."

Qarl nodded, squaring his tiny shoulders as if he fully embraced the responsibility. "Good luck!" he called after us as the Queen and I approached the double doors of the throne room.

We certainly needed all the luck we could get. The moment we had traveled so far for was finally upon us. I sucked in my breath, more than a bit nervous. I had rehearsed my persuasive speech in my head many times on our journey, but the time for practice was over. It was go time, and I hoped that I wouldn't screw anything up. Without further ado, the Hob Goblins thrust open the doors of the throne room, and we entered.

The throne room looked as though it had seen better days. The entire chamber was in disarray. Gadgets were littered about, furniture was overturned, and cobwebs filled the corners. Traces of former opulence could be seen beneath the layer of chaos, but the pathetic current state of the room overpowered any royal detail that may have lingered. The space reminded me of my bedroom as a teenager.

A corpulent alien reclined on a large cushioned throne. Thick, scaly blue skin covered his entire body. He possessed an oddly shaped head with a single tiny horn poking straight out the top. A hooked nose, thick purple lips, multiple chin folds, and an elongated forehead rounded out the creature's face.

The Queen curtsied, and I bowed. "Great Leader," the Queen began. "I am pleased to be able to visit your beautiful home at long last. You must be Asdf."

She proffered her hand, but Asdf ignored it with a rude scoff. He seemed much more interested in me, scanning me up and down with an intrigued look in his large eyes.

"Hey, Jkl!" Asdf shouted in a booming voice.

"What?" a distant voice in an adjoining room called back.

"Come here!"

"Leave me alone," Jkl responded. "I'm playing with a planet in Middle Space."

"Jkl, come on! It's an Earth-namuH!" Asdf exclaimed.

"It's a what?"

"Earth-Human! Cut me a break, you know I'm dysleqsic."

"So am I, dude. You say there's an Earth-Human here? Hold on, I'm coming!"

A moment later, another large blue alien lumbered into the throne room and seated himself on an empty throne next to his fellow leader. He looked identical to Asdf. His eyes lit up when he saw me, but his face fell almost immediately when he noticed the Queen.

"What is *she* doing here?" he asked Asdf, the disgust in his voice plain.

"She hasn't said yet," Asdf replied with a shrug. "But check out the Earth-Human! Isn't he great? We haven't seen one up close in many mirqrulls."

"That we haven't. Tell me," Jkl said, addressing me directly. "What is Earth like to live on?"

I won't bore you, the reader, with my description of Earth, since you presumably live there as well, but suffice it to say that my words held Asdf and Jkl in rapt attention. The Queen waited patiently while I spoke to the two Great Leaders of the "magnificent splendor" of Earth. At one point, Asdf stopped me.

"Wait, wait!" he cried. "I must take notes of this!" He plucked the horn from his head and began using it as a pencil, excitedly taking notes right to left on a scrap of paper that he produced from one of his many skin folds.

"As you can see," I concluded at last, "Earth is a very unique planet."

"Quite, quite!" Asdf and Jkl agreed in unison.

"But now I must share the real reason for my visiting this corner of the cosmos." *Here I go!* I took a deep breath.

"You mean Qorner of the Qosmos," Jkl corrected. I blinked, not expecting the strange interruption.

"Well," I continued, collecting my thoughts, "the true purpose for my visit regards the planet X@X."

A cloud passed over Jkl's face. "*She* put you up to this, didn't she?" He nodded disdainfully toward the Queen, who stood silently by.

My stomach sank. "I was asked to—"

"Ugh! I knew it," Jkl interrupted. "I do not want to hear any more. Go away, both of you. Let us get back to our games."

This wasn't going the way I had planned. I didn't know what to say. To my relief, the Queen stepped forward. "We ask that you listen to our request, Great Leaders."

"We know what you will ask," Asdf retorted, exasperation growing in his voice. "By Hob! You will stop at nothing to seize power from us. You have brought an Earth-Human here to manipulate us into saving your little kingdom planet!"

"So you do intend to destroy it?"

"That's right. We intend to be rid of it. You are a throne stealer. Why should you have a home?"

The Queen drew herself up to her full height. "Your Leaderships," she began, "I have no interest in taking your thrones. The only reason I am in power is to take care of the universe that your careless actions have often left in disorderly condition. Someone must bring order to space if you will not. Why do you resent my efforts?"

"Insidious insurrection is your aim," Asdf responded, thrusting an accusing finger in her direction. "We know you are a witch. You cursed your own sister to increase your power."

"I did what I had to for the good of the universe, as I always have, and as I will continue to do."

"Even if that were true, why should we keep your planet around?" Jkl chimed in. "It has long had no use to us, and we have wanted to throw it away for quite some time now. It is an ugly misshapen thing that we cannot play with."

"Must everything in the cosmos be played with?" asked the Queen. It was a valid, if risky, question.

"It's Qosmos!" Asdf roared. "Ugh, why are Humans so stupid?" A flash of anger crossed the Queen's face at the insult, but I was focused on something else. Something was oddly familiar about these two aliens, but I couldn't put my finger on it.

At that moment, a Hob Goblin entered the room and approached the two thrones. In a hushed whisper, it appeared to be telling the two Great Leaders something important.

"He's back?" Asdf asked, his voice lowered.

"Why of course! That little genius!" Jkl exclaimed softly. "Why is he waiting outside? Send him in!"

The Hob Goblin nodded and stepped through the doorway, returning a moment later with…Qarl!

"Welcome back, Qarl!" the two aliens bellowed in unison as Qarl entered the chamber timidly.

"You brilliant blue bastard!" Jkl cried. "I should've known this was your doing."

"You've delivered her right into our hands. Well done!" Asdf exclaimed.

I couldn't believe my eyes and ears. *Qarl? A double agent this entire time?* I tried to catch his eye, looking frantically for some sort of explanation, but he avoided my gaze, standing by the two thrones with a sheepish look on his face.

The realization spread over me in a sickening wave. It was all making sense now: the dysleqsia, the blue skin, the horn pencil, the obsession with the letter *Q*. He was one of them! Qarl had had a major hand in planning this whole adventure. Of course this had been his plan all along.

I was hurt and angry all at once. How could Qarl betray us like this? How could we not have seen it coming? What fools we had been!

I didn't have time to be angry long, however. After a moment, the shock and rage were replaced by a gripping fear. What would happen to us now? We were sitting right where the Great Leaders wanted us, trapped in their domain and powerless against their army of Hob Goblins. The situation was getting out of our hands and into their clutches.

I glanced over at the Queen and was unsettled to see that her usually serene face was contorted with a mixture of confusion and disbelief.

"We obviously are rejecting your request to spare your precious planet," Jkl spoke up. "Your time here is wasted."

"But perhaps we don't send you away," Asdf pondered aloud, a fiendish grin spreading across his face. "Qarl has brought us a golden opportunity. Maybe we should deal with you now once and for all while we have the chance!"

He rose from his throne and took a thundering step toward us. I knew I needed to do something. The time for reasoning with them was over.

Then a thought struck me. If Qarl was from Hob, then Asdf and Jkl should be size shifters as well, and if that was the case, well then…

I reached into my pocket, my hand closing around the rubber eraser Qarl had taken from my bedroom. I slowly withdrew it, turning it over in my fingers as I considered my next move. Asdf was coming closer.

Without a second thought, I drew my arm back, took aim, and thrust the eraser straight at Asdf's head. It hit him square in the forehead with a little *boink,* then bounced off and struck Jkl on the arm.

For a moment, time froze. I was sure I had just signed my death sentence.

Then, with a hiss, Asdf and Jkl began to shrink. I grabbed the Queen and shouted, "Let's go!" as I ran toward the exit.

Behind me, Asdf and Jkl called out as they continued shrinking. "Seize them!"

As we flew past the guards and the rest of our party in the entryway, we yelled at our companions to run. No doubt confused, they nonetheless took off at our heels while dozens of Hob Goblins poured out of every corner of the palace and gave chase.

We ducked down hallways and through empty rooms, but our luck was running out. There seemed to be an infinite number of Hob Goblins chasing us.

Our group raced into a storage room and shut the door, hearts pounding. We backed into a dark corner and stayed silent, hoping the rapidly approaching footsteps would pass us by.

I could hear the Goblin grunts coming closer and closer. The footsteps stopped outside the door, and, for an interminable moment, all I could sense was my heart pounding in my ears, so loud I was afraid it would be heard by our pursuers.

Suddenly, the door flew open with a crash, and we were faced with the sharp ends of dozens of daggers. We were cornered. There was no way to escape.

As the Goblins grunted with glee, Asdf and Jkl shuffled across the doorway of the storage room, back to their original size. Qarl was nowhere in sight. I wondered where the little traitor had gone.

"Take them to the Edge of the Universe!" the Great Leaders thundered.

At daggerpoint, our group was taken to the long hallway and forced into the telepod. A Hob Goblin punched in some coordinates, and we took a final dizzying trip.

Once we arrived at our destination, we were pushed rudely out of the pod. Asdf and Jkl followed shortly afterward. Using their daggers to goad us, the Goblins forced us into a single-file line with me at the head.

We found ourselves outdoors, standing at the edge of a cliff and looking out into the infinite blackness of space. Not a single star twinkled in the sky beyond. A bitter, howling wind cut through my clothes and wrapped itself around my bones, chilling me to my core.

"We are at the Edge of the Universe," Bobby whispered to me over my shoulder. I looked back at him and nodded wordlessly.

Before us stood a lone doorway with no door, only a wooden support framing the murky darkness. One of the Hob Goblins pressed a button on a remote it held in its hand. Fog began to fill the doorway until anything beyond was completely obscured.

This must be the portal! I realized, my stomach tightening. *I'm actually about to be banished!* My mind raced back over everything I had been told about this place of punishment, trying to mentally prepare myself for what was about to happen. Qarl and the Queen had tried to assuage my fear of the portal in the past, but Qarl had turned out to be a conniving liar, and the Queen naïve for trusting him. Perhaps this place was really as terrible as so many believed it was. Whatever the truth was about the portal, however, I wasn't going to have to wonder long.

"Earth-Human, you are sentenced to be banished through The Portal Beyond Which No Man Awaits," Asdf and Jkl proclaimed in unison. "Step through the door!"

I turned to look behind me one last time and caught the Queen's tear-filled eye. She nodded gently as I mouthed "I'm so sorry" to her. I had tried and failed. X@X's future was all but sealed, and my companions were about to be banished forever. There was nothing left for me to do.

I turned and stepped into the swirling fog.

π π π π π

I walked through the dense mists for what felt like an eternity. Finally the fog began to dissolve into thin wisps, and I could see my way ahead.

I was walking on a cobblestone street, which was lined with quaint little houses. Each house was surrounded by a small yard containing trees, grass, and a well-tended garden overflowing with colorful flowers. I was surprised to discover that I seemed to be in the center of a beautiful village. However, it was who I saw that shocked me the most.

Everywhere I looked, I saw aliens. Some were hard at work, tending to gardens and mowing lawns, while others milled about, engaging in conversations with each other. Every creature wore a bright smile, and tinkling laughter could be heard drifting up the street. It was a happy atmosphere, to be sure.

I was confused. Qarl had told me that no one could see or interact with anyone else. Why, then, was a sea of aliens greeting my eyes? It was just as well, I told myself. Qarl had proven himself to be an untrustworthy liar. He had likely lied about this as well.

I continued walking down the street in awe, gazing at the beauty around me. Each house was painted a distinctive hue, each garden contained different flowers, and each bush was trimmed in a unique pattern. Music wafted through the air as one alien reclined on his front porch, playing a viotar. Everything seemed truly peaceful.

Suddenly, I heard footsteps behind me on the stones. I turned to look back the way I had come, peering through the fog that still cascaded down the street. Then, as I watched in disbelief, I saw a figure emerge from the mists. It was…

Chapter Q

…Qarl?

"Qarl!" I exclaimed in shock, my mouth agape. I couldn't believe he was here. My incredulity was quickly replaced by anger, however. *How dare he show his betraying face so boldly after what happened!*

My eyes narrowed. "Why, you little blue bastard!" I growled at him, marching over to where he stood, my hands ready to throttle him.

"Hold it!" he shouted. "Don't hurt me. I come in peace."

"And you're gonna leave in pieces!" I shot back. I grabbed Qarl by the neck and lowered my head until my eyes were level with his. "I can't believe I trusted you, Qarl. You betrayed me. You betrayed all of us!"

Qarl laughed aloud. "No, I didn't," he protested. "Look, I can explain everything. Just let go of me."

I released my grip on his wrinkled neck, but I wasn't about to let him off the hook. "What's to explain?" I countered. "You're one of them. You ditched me when I needed you most. And you let me get banished here without doing a thing about it. Some friend you turned out to be."

Qarl crossed his arms and glared up at me. "Well if it isn't just like you to jump to conclusions. You Earth-Humans are impossible!"

"What other conclusions could I possibly come to, you blue freak!" I shouted at him. "Do you deny that you're one of them, that you were born and raised on Hob, that you're one of their kind?"

"Of course I don't deny it," Qarl replied. "So what? I don't recall that being a crime."

"So you were in their pocket the whole time. You hid your identity, infiltrated X@X, gained the Queen's confidence, and convinced her to make this trip to Hob…all so you could help Asdf and Jkl destroy us once and for all."

"Boy, you're really stupid, aren't you?" Qarl retorted. "If Asdf and Jkl really want to destroy X@X, don't you think They could do it without my help? They could purge X@X from Their playground without luring anybody to Their planet. In fact, I think They'd prefer it if most of us stayed away from Hob. They don't like visitors very much, as I'm sure you've found out by now."

"Yes, I'm well aware of that fact, thanks to you," I spat back.

"Thanks to me? You think I had something to do with this because I happen to be of the same species as Asdf and Jkl?" He jabbed his bony finger at me. "You're just looking for a reason to distrust me, aren't you? Some friend *you* turned out to be!"

"Well, Qarl, you're kind of handing me these reasons on silver platters, you know," I replied, my voice dripping with sarcasm. "It's not like I'm digging deep for them."

"Every door has two sides, as does every story. If you'd just shut up and let me explain myself, you'd understand everything. Why do you think I'm here right now? To taunt you?" I shrugged, and Qarl shook his head. "No, I'm here to help you. Just listen to me, all right?"

I was still seething inside but ultimately decided to see if my former companion could explain his way out of this one. Besides, it's not like I didn't have all the time in the universe on my hands to sit and listen. Being banished for life really opens up your schedule.

I sighed and sat down on a rock. "Fine, go ahead," I said reluctantly. "Impress me with your spin on what happened."

Qarl plopped down in the dirt in front of me, his face showing eagerness to set me straight. "Yes, it's true that I'm originally from Hob," he began. "From a very young age, my natural intelligence and propensity for understanding technology landed me a good position working for Asdf and Jkl."

"See?" I interrupted, glaring at him. "I knew it!"

"Oh, shut up," Qarl replied sharply. "Yes, I worked for the Great Leaders of Hob at one time. But I soon became dissatisfied with Their lazy and apathetic way of running things. As an alien working for the rulers of the entire Universe, I craved experiences, knowledge, excitement, and challenges…and Hob offered none of those. Most of my time was spent designing different ways for Asdf and Jkl to indulge in Their stupid games. I must've engineered hundreds of different comet boosters and magnetic planet shifters." He chuckled as he recalled these former days.

"So what did you do then?" I asked, my interest growing slightly.

"I decided to leave Hob," he continued. "Not only was I bored with what life on Hob had to offer, but I was becoming concerned with Asdf and Jkl's leadership as well. It was bordering on irresponsible, and I didn't wish to contribute to it any longer. So I left."

"Where did you go?" I wondered curiously.

"I became nomadic for a while. I explored many a planet throughout Space, meeting both aliens and Humans. I had many memorable experiences, which I won't bore you with now, but suffice it to say that life was definitely far more exciting than it had been on stuffy old Hob. Only one thing was missing."

"Love," I said with a mischievous smirk.

"No, not love!" Qarl retorted, looking at me as if I were an idiot. "Purpose."

"Purpose?"

"Yes. My experiences were amazing and all, but I had no purpose, no goal, no driving force to make the whole wonderful journey mean something. Don't get me wrong: the moment-by-moment experience of Life is as important as anything, but sometimes it's keeping sight of a goal that makes the journey more bearable and meaningful. After all, you Earth-Humans wouldn't love Fridays were it not for Saturdays, right?"

"And so you found love, and *that* became your purpose," I chortled. Qarl reached up and smacked me on the head.

"Of course not, stupid," he replied. "There's more to life than love, you know."

My loveless life sure hoped so.

"The Queen of the Cosmos had already long assumed power by the time I left Hob," Qarl continued. "After exploring much of her realm, I began to witness for myself what a great leader she was. It was clear that she cared about the Universe, keeping peace and order while the lazy Leaders of Hob did Their own thing off in Hyper Space.

"I eventually decided that I wanted to meet this Queen and perhaps serve in her employ. I desired a purpose, and helping the Queen of the Cosmos protect the Universe seemed as good a purpose as any. So I moved to X@X, and I've been there ever since."

"You kept your origins a secret though, didn't you?" I pressed, making sure he didn't leave out this crucial detail.

Qarl nodded. "Yes. Yes, I did."

"Why?"

"It wasn't for the reasons you think. You see, I knew from my extensive travels that some in the Universe distrusted the Great Leaders of Hob. Many of the aliens outright feared Them, in fact. X@X especially was a place full of these inclinations, as it was the Queen's residence, and she distrusted Them more than anybody…for reasons you well know."

I nodded. Qarl stood up and began pacing while he continued his narrative. "So you see, I couldn't reveal where I was from. X@X would have distrusted me from the beginning, and I never would have been able to work for the Queen. I didn't want Hob to haunt me for the rest of my life and stunt my chances at a better future, so I kept quiet about it. Besides, it's not like my heritage is something I'm particularly proud of. It's just one facet of my life, one early step in my journey."

"I see," I replied, still unsure of what to make of this. Qarl stopped in front of me and placed his hand on my shoulder.

"My allegiance lies with the Queen," he assured me. "Please believe that. I can't help where I started. I can only help where I am now."

I looked up into his big eyes staring steadily into mine. I wanted to trust him again. I really did. I just didn't know what to think anymore.

"This all…may be true," I told him. "But that doesn't explain why you left me alone to be banished, why you only showed up now when it's too late."

Qarl grinned at me. "Silly Human," he said. "Who says it's too late?"

"Um, everybody who knows anything about this place." I gestured around me.

"Well," Qarl replied smugly, "that's because they don't know how the portal works like I do."

"You know a way to get out of here?" I asked, confused by what he was implying.

"Of course I do. You think I would have followed you in here if I didn't know how to get back out again? I'm not *that* selfless!" He chuckled as he said this.

"Well, thanks a heap," I retorted, rolling my eyes. "But, seriously, how the hell do you know how to escape from here? Nobody else seems to."

There was a momentary pause. Qarl seemed reluctant to answer.

"Qarl," I pressed, "how do you know?"

"Um, that would be because I…um…helped build the portal." Qarl looked down and shuffled his feet, as if he sensed my response would be a negative one. He was right.

"You *what*!?!" I shouted. "You helped Asdf and Jkl build this place of punishment? I *knew* you guys were in cahoots!"

"Oh, please don't start that again," Qarl protested. "This happened when I was young, before I had traveled and gained a better perspective on the Universe. Hob was all I knew. I was just following orders."

"This explains why you knew so much about it when I asked you in the desert," I realized, my mind piecing together the puzzle. Qarl nodded.

"I was one of the designers, actually," he admitted. "I knew technology very well, so I was commissioned to come up with some sort of multidimensional portal that Asdf and Jkl could use for banishment and intimidation purposes."

I shook my head in stunned disbelief. "I can't believe you helped construct one of the most feared things in the entire universe. Do you have trouble sleeping at night?"

"I sleep just fine, thank you very much," Qarl retorted instinctively, before lowering his voice. "Like I told you before, my past with Hob is something I'm not exactly proud of, but it happened, and I can't change that."

I turned and took a few steps away. I was having trouble processing the fact that my little blue companion had been the mastermind behind the thing that kept so many gripped in fear, the thing that now held me and so many others captive. Those aliens I had seen when I first passed through the portal…those poor creatures were doomed because of what Qarl had done. My mind shuddered to think of how many others were exiled on other dimensions of this plane, all because of Qarl.

"The portal was never meant for aliens, you know," a soft voice behind me spoke, as if reading my thoughts. I turned around: Qarl had followed me. "It wasn't meant for any of us aliens."

"Who was it meant for, then?" I asked wearily.

"Humans," he replied. "Like the Queen. Like those on X@X. Even like you." Qarl stepped closer, his face earnest. "The portal was commissioned soon after she cursed her sister. Asdf and Jkl were afraid of her. She was a Human—a powerful one—and They wanted to control her kind before her kind could control Them.

"The portal was designed for Humans, to intimidate them so that they would never dare challenge the authority and position of the Great Leaders of Hob. That's why you can see aliens here and they can see you. The multidimensional aspect of the portal was only designed to apply to Humans.

"Don't you see? It's called The Portal Beyond Which No *Man* Awaits. This place was never meant to house aliens."

"So why are there aliens here, then?" I asked.

"Asdf and Jkl's plan backfired. As I'm sure you know by now, aliens tend to be a fearful species. News of the portal had the unintended result of invoking fear in the alien population of the Universe, while Humans remained largely unaffected.

"You see, aliens fear loneliness above all else. Humans, on the other hand, fear many different things, and Asdf and Jkl did not realize this when They designed the portal. They constructed it to play on the fear of loneliness, for that is what They knew, but there are a number of Humans to whom the prospect of being alone would be quite welcome."

I nodded. "But what about the humans that *do* fear loneliness? Surely the portal would have an effect on them."

"It would, if Humans were intent on marching on Hob and overthrowing the Great Leaders. But such is not the case. Asdf and Jkl are aliens too, remember, and Their propensity toward extreme and irrational fear is as strong as any alien's. They don't realize that Humans don't pose much of a threat. Most Humans I've encountered don't wish to rule the Universe, and those that do are already convinced that they are doing so. The Queen is the only one who poses a credible threat to Hob, and she would only take extreme measures if necessary."

"And she doesn't fear the portal," I mused.

"If she does, that fear doesn't stop her," Qarl replied. "And so that is why this place is almost entirely populated with aliens, banished here by Asdf and Jkl. The Great

Leaders didn't really have a choice if They wanted to keep up appearances. Their intimidation plan was already failing, and They couldn't afford to feed into that failure. Desperate to be taken seriously, They were forced to banish aliens from time to time—in hopes that Humans would see this and begin to recognize the seriousness of the threat—but the portal was never designed for our kind."

"Why haven't you helped them escape?" I asked him.

"Well, it's not like I've been around to do so, have I?" Qarl responded.

I shrugged. *I suppose not.*

"Besides, look around you," Qarl continued. "This place isn't all that bad. The aliens have built a real civilization here."

"It's actually quite beautiful," I admitted. "And the aliens I saw seemed remarkably happy and at peace."

"I bet if you asked most of these aliens if they wanted to go back, they'd say no. This place is a paradise. Their worst fear has become their safe home. Why should they go back to the other side now?"

"I suppose you're right," I reluctantly conceded. "But what about the humans banished here? Do they want to escape?"

"There aren't many here to begin with," Qarl replied. "You're one of the first."

"And they're not really alone, are they? They can hang out with the aliens at least, even if the humans can't see one another."

"Exactly. So maybe they too are ok with staying."

"Maybe. But one thing is certain. *I* would like to get out of here. Can you show me how?"

With a nod, Qarl turned on his heel and motioned for me to follow him. We headed further up the cobblestone path, turned a bend, and entered an orchard.

"Unfortunately, you will not be able to leave this place by the way that I came in," Qarl explained as we walked. "You're not a size shifter, and the secret entrance I used is quite tiny. I, on the other hand, can make myself as small as I like, which definitely helps. You can never be too small to fit in a hole."

"What is that last part supposed to mean?"

"Must I explain everything to you?" Qarl asked with familiar exasperation. "It's just an expression. If you can't fit in a hole, it's always because you're too large to fit in the hole, never because you're too small."

"Oh. I see," I replied. "So what am I supposed to do, then?"

"You'll have to use the regular route out of here."

"There's a regular route out of here?"

Qarl grinned. "Asdf and Jkl don't know about it, but yes. When I built the portal, I programmed a way for anybody to escape should they want to. It's just up to them to figure out how."

"I take it that no one has figured it out yet, huh?" I ventured. "One would think that news of that would travel pretty quickly through the universe, not to mention the truth of what lies beyond the portal."

"You are correct," Qarl acknowledged. "No one has discovered the escape…or if they have, they have failed in their attempts to use it. My hidden programming must've been more complex than I thought."

"Maybe some of them just declined to use it," I postulated. "The aliens at least seem happy here."

"That's possible," Qarl mused. His face took on an odd expression, as if he was simultaneously proud of the fact that his encryption had been so clever as to escape notice yet regretful of the failed attempt to help others leave this place.

I grinned at the conflicting emotions chasing themselves across my companion's face. "It's the thought that counts," I told him reassuringly. "And it wasn't for nothing: today I'll get to use your ultrasecret escape method."

Qarl brightened at this and quickened his pace as we neared the center of the orchard. After a moment, he stopped abruptly. He looked around, seemingly unsure of himself.

"What? What's going on?" I asked him.

"I'm just trying to make sure we're going the right way. This scenery doesn't look completely familiar."

"Don't tell me the 'Great Traveler of the Universe' is lost in his own creation," I remarked sarcastically. "Wouldn't that be a hoot, you stuck in here with me for all of eternity?" I chuckled.

"Don't count on it. I can always go back the way I came," Qarl retorted haughtily. "Remember, it's *your* ass we're trying to save right now. I can always leave you behind if things fall through."

The smile melted off my face. "Please don't."

Qarl smirked and pushed past me into the trees beyond. We had only gone a few feet when we stopped abruptly once again.

"Aha! There it is!" Qarl announced triumphantly. "I knew it was around here somewhere." There, in a clearing ahead, stood the largest and oldest tree I had ever seen in my life.

"You're telling me a *tree* is my ticket out of here?" I asked incredulously. And what a weird tree it was. A massive trunk supported hundreds of gnarly branches, while thick roots snaked along the ground at its base. No leaves were to be seen, only blackened twigs that looked as if they had been through a fire. The tree creaked a welcome as we approached it slowly.

"This tree contains the key that will unlock the portal door," Qarl explained. "Simply press the correct button and select the correct key, and freedom will be yours. Careful, though—pick the wrong key and they all go up in flames." Well, that explained the scorched branches.

I approached the tree eagerly, ready to be free of this place, beautiful as it was. Just then, I remembered something.

"Where are the Queen and the others?" I asked.

"They've been banished as well, and I'm helping them to—oh fuq!" Qarl exclaimed.

"What now?"

"I told the Queen I would check back on her mirkrons ago! Our fight kept me here longer than intended. I really need to go now." He began to run back the way he had come.

"But wait! How will I get out of here?"

"It's easy!" he called back over his shoulder. "Just press the button and pick the key. You'll figure it out!" Before I could say a word, he disappeared into the trees.

I stood there, my mouth hanging open. I couldn't believe Qarl had just left me again. *His instructions better get me out of here, or else!* I thought.

Turning back to the tree in front of me, I stepped closer to locate the buttons. There were two embedded in the gnarled trunk in front of me. One read "Here," and the other read "Press here." *Tricky*. Hoping and trusting my instinct, eventually my finger reached out and depressed the right button. A loud click was heard.

No sooner had I pressed the button than a thousand keys instantly appeared on the ends of the blackened branches. Shining in the light, waving gently in the breeze, each key had a number engraved in its shaft. Red keys and blue keys and green keys and yellow keys—like a rainbow these shimmering objects doused the tree in color.

I knew which key was mine. Eagerly I reached up and grasped it.

Suddenly, over my body washed a dazzling light. Next thing I remember is being back at my desk in my bedroom at home, pondering both how I managed to get back there and what had happened to my new friends.

As I slowly rose from my desk—going downstairs to ask Mom for more brownies—everything within me knew one thing for certain: 27 Sickamore Street and I would never be the same again.

END

(...continue reading...)

Epilogue

If you are currently feeling a mixture of dismay, frustration, or even anger, I completely understand. The truth is that you know as much as I do about the whole situation. As of this writing, I still haven't heard from Qarl, Bobby, the Queen, or anyone else I met on my little adventure. I have no idea if everyone escaped the portal, or even if X@X survived the purge. Once I know more, I will be sure to let you in on the details.

In the meantime, I have secreted the answer to which key opens the portal within the pages of this manuscript. How can you find it, you ask? Start "here."

www.ingramcontent.com/pod-product-compliance
Lightning Source LLC
Chambersburg PA
CBHW021123110726
47900CB00007B/2310

9781734601503